# so hard
# to say

# so hard to say

## ALEX SANCHEZ

SIMON PULSE
New York   London   Toronto   Sydney

This book is a work of fiction. Any references to historical events, real people, or real locales are used fictitiously. Other names, characters, places, and incidents are the product of the author's imagination, and any resemblance to actual events or locales or persons, living or dead, is entirely coincidental.

SIMON PULSE
An imprint of Simon & Schuster Children's Publishing Division
1230 Avenue of the Americas, New York, NY 10020
Copyright © 2004 by Alex Sanchez
All rights reserved, including the right of reproduction in whole or in
part in any form.
SIMON PULSE and colophon are trademarks of Simon & Schuster, Inc.
Also available in Simon and Schuster Books for Young Readers
hardcover edition.
The text of this book was set in Didot LH.
Manufactured in the United States of America
First SIMON PULSE edition May 2006
10 9 8 7 6 5 4 3 2 1
The Library of Congress has cataloged the hardcover edition as follows:
Sanchez, Alex.
So hard to say / Alex Sanchez.—1st ed.
p. cm.
Summary: Thirteen-year-old Xio, a Mexican-American girl, and Frederick, who has just moved to California from Wisconsin, quickly become close friends, but when Xio starts thinking of Frederick as her boyfriend, he must confront his feelings of confusion and face the fear that he might be gay.
ISBN-13: 978-0-689-86564-0 (hc.)
ISBN-10: 0-689-86564-3 (hc.)
[1. Homosexuality—Fiction. 2. Mexican-Americans—Fiction. 3. Interpersonal relations—Fiction. 4. Schools—Fiction. 5. California—Fiction.] I. Title.
PZ7.S19475Fr 2004      [Fic]—dc22    2003021128
ISBN-13: 978-1-4169-1189-0 (pbk.)
ISBN-10: 1-4169-1189-8 (pbk.)

*To friendship—in all its wondrous forms.*

# Acknowledgments

With gratitude to my editor, David Gale; my agent, Miriam Altshuler; and all those who contributed to the creation of this book with their encouragement and feedback, including Bruce Aufhammer, Lindsay Brown, Bill Brockschmidt, Alexandra Cooper, Kim Feldman, the Fine Arts Work Center of Provincetown, Kate Goldbaum, James Howe, Jason Hungerford, Chuck Jones, J. R. Key, Erica Lazaro, Kevin Lewis, Pablo Madriz, Elizabeth McCracken, Rob Phelps, George Pierson, John Porter, J. Q. Quiñones, Bob Ripperger, Tim Rogan, Cosper Scafidi, Ian Terry, the Virginia Center for Creative Arts, Mike Walker, Bob Witeck, and Jacqueline Woodson. Thank you all.

# Chapter 1

## Xio

My name is (drum roll, please) María Xiomara Iris Juárez Hidalgo, but nobody calls me María. For short, I just go by Xio—pronounced *C.O.* It rhymes with Leo, my sign. Like most Leos, my best quality is my unfailing loyalty. I'm utterly devoted to my friends. . . . and of course, to me.

Just kidding. Well, maybe it's a little true. Madonna is a Leo. (Yes!) So was Napoleon. We love to conquer and take charge, plus we're generous, fun, openhearted and love to speak our minds.

On the downside, we love to speak our minds. Sometimes it gets me into deep, deep *caca*. Then if I tell Mami about it, she laughs and says I need to learn to keep my mouth shut.

"But that's totally impossible," I tell her. "When I've got something to say, I have to say it."

My other faults: I can be pretty lazy when it comes to housework. Like on weekends? My all-time

1

favorite thing is to laze in bed, talking on the phone with friends—hopping from one call to the next. I think Call Waiting is the best invention ever.

But then Mami comes in and makes me get off the phone to do chores. "You need to learn the world doesn't revolve around you," she says, which makes no sense.

"If the world doesn't revolve around me," I argue, "then why do I have to get out of bed?"

Mami shakes her head and rolls her eyes heavenward, asking God for *paciencia*.

"Okay . . ." Climbing from bed, I give her a big hug. Sometimes I wonder how Mami handles being a single mom. I know I can be pretty high maintenance. But Mami's strong, in a quiet way. I don't know if I could ever be that strong. . . . or that quiet.

Both Mami and Papi are from Mexico, but they met here in California. I remember when I was little Papi used to stand me on his shoes and dance me around the living room as mariachi trumpets blared on the radio. Mami would wave her arms, warning him to be careful. Then he'd reach out for her too, all of us dancing together with me tucked between them.

When I was seven, my little brother—Esteban Jesús Francisco (Stevie for short)—was born. He's a pain in the butt, always getting into my stuff (a typical curious Aquarius), but I love him. He looks a lot like Papi, with lighter skin than mine.

I look more like Mami. We're both *morenas*—with skin that's golden colored. But I'm more *chata* than Mami. That means I have a flat, catlike nose—which I hate. My best feature is my hair—thick and black. Mami calls it my mane.

I was seven when Mami and Papi broke up. It came gradually, not with yelling or fights, but with a lot of rumblings and low voices. I remember putting my ear to their bedroom door, trying to figure out what was going on and wondering, *Was it because of something I'd done?*

I've asked Mami a million times why Papi left. Was he in love with another woman? Didn't he love us anymore? But the only thing she says is, "Your papi and I had differences."

"Like, what's that supposed to mean?"

Mami sighs. "It means that sometimes, no matter how much two people love each other, they just aren't meant to be together. When you're older you'll understand."

I hate it when she says things like that.

Papi moved north to San Francisco. At first he'd phone me every day. I'd run home after school to hear his voice. But slowly his calls became once a week. Then one time a month. Then only Christmas and my birthday. I begged to visit him but he wouldn't let me. Instead he visited us once a year, but last year he didn't even do that.

When I turned thirteen last August I didn't go out of the house, hoping he'd call. As usual, Mami threw a party for me and all my friends came. Every time the phone rang I jumped for it, certain it would be Papi. But it wasn't.

That night after everybody left, I went to my room and stared at my nightstand's Little Mermaid lamp. Mami says Papi got it for me on my second birthday.

Across the shade swim tropical fish, a little faded now. The stem is Ariel with her long flowing hair, sitting on a porcelain wave. Her green tail curves around an empty space where a clock used to be. When it stopped working Papi took it to find a replacement, but before finding a new clock he left.

The lamp looks kind of weird with Ariel sitting on an empty space. I've tried to fill the space with stuff. Once I wedged in a little tray filled with chocolates, but that lasted about two seconds, before I ate them all. I'm a total chocoholic. It's my favorite comfort food.

I could've used some the night of my party. When Mami came in and put her arm around me I burst into tears, burying my head in her shoulder. "He doesn't love me anymore."

"Shh," Mami whispered. "That's not true. You're the daughter he always wanted."

Yeah, right. "I don't care if he never calls again!"

In the month since then, I've rehearsed in my mind every day for when—or if?—he phones. "I don't want you to ever call again!" I'm going to tell him. I really will. I mean it.

Anyway, enough about him. Back to me: I'm in eighth grade at San Cayetano Middle. Classes started two weeks ago. And today a new boy arrived in first period—white, kind of small, with kick-butt blue eyes and sandy blond hair spiked in front that made me want to whoosh my fingers through it. Of course, I didn't. At least not yet. But hello! I'm thirteen already. Where's my boyfriend? I'm waiting!

Ms. Marciano (that's Spanish for "martian") introduced the new guy as Fred.

Big mistake.

"Excuse me," he told her. "But, um, my name's not Fred or Freddy or Rick, or Ricky. It's *Frederick*."

Ms. Martian stared at him like she was peering out of a spaceship.

"Okay, *Frederick*. Can you take a seat beside Xio, please?" She pointed to the empty desk next to me. My best friend, Carmen, had sat there till we got split up for talking too much—after only *two* days. How unfair was *that*?

While Frederick-not-Fred weaved between rows, Carmen gave me a huge grin from across the room. She kids me because I seem to always go for shorter guys. But can I help it if most boys my age are so shrimpy?

"Hi," I whispered as Frederick slid into the desk beside me.

"Um . . . hi." A cute little smile crept across his face. He has really pretty lips, too—kind of pouty.

Ms. Visitor from the Red Planet started babbling something for the class to write down. Frederick pulled out his pen but the ink wouldn't come out. He rubbed the ballpoint on his paper till he practically gouged a hole in it, without saying anything. He must be shy. I know if I needed a pen I would've stopped the entire class.

"Here," I told him, holding mine out. "I have an extra."

"Xio?" Ms. Space Alien scolded. "Can you pay attention, please?"

"I'm lending him a pen," I shouted and handed it to him.

Everyone had turned to stare at us, and Frederick was apple red. But after everybody glanced away again, he looked at me and whispered, "Thanks."

Oh, my God, I love his eyes.

Tonight at dinner while scooping some *arroz con*

*pollo* onto Stevie's plate I told Mami, "I want to get blue contact lenses."

"Oh, don't be silly." Mami passed me the bread. "Your eyes are beautiful just as they are."

"But I'm so bored with brown eyes. They're so unoriginal. Everyone in the world I know has brown eyes."

At least until today.

# Chapter 2

## Frederick

The pen girl (I couldn't figure out her name) reminds me of my best friend back home, Janice — funny, smart, nice hair, and kind of loud, but in a good way.

It's always been easier for me to make friends with girls. I'm not sure why.

I did say hi to a couple of guys today, but they only replied, "'Sup?" and turned away as if I was weird for talking to them.

It's the opposite of my school in Wisconsin, where I knew almost everybody. We'd all grown up together. I couldn't walk three steps down the hall without someone talking to me. Here everyone already has their own cliques.

I wish we hadn't moved. What if I never make any friends?

It would probably help if I spoke Spanish, since so many people here are Mexican. They constantly switch languages. The only thing I know how to say is Taco Bell. I doubt that would score me any points.

At lunch I looked for Pen Girl but she sat surrounded by her friends. It felt too strange to just carry my tray up and ask, "Hey, can I sit with you?"

So instead I ended up sitting by myself—and feeling like a freak.

After lunch, on the way to my locker, I did notice this one Mexican boy who looked friendly. He was laughing with a group of girls and was small like me, except tan, with brown hair and eyes—and dimples in his cheeks. I'm not sure what attracted my attention to him. Sometimes I just notice people.

He saw me and did a double take, like he thought I was somebody he knew. I glanced over my shoulder thinking maybe he was looking at someone else. But when I gazed back he was still staring at me, his dimples growing even deeper as his grin grew wider.

My heart started racing and my chest tightening. Suddenly I wanted to leave. But why? Hadn't I wanted to talk to another guy? Yeah, but there was something about him. I wasn't sure what.

Just then a bunch of rowdy boys walked by, hissing and hooting at Dimple Guy in Spanish. Although I didn't know what they were saying, from the way they waved their wrists I could guess they were calling him gay.

Dimple Dude yelled something back at the boys as they swaggered past. And I hurried to my locker thinking, *What if I'd been caught talking to him?* That would've been suicide, especially my first day at a new school.

At the end of the day Mom picked me up. "Hi, honey. How did it go?"

"It sucked," I told her, climbing into the car.

Of course, that sent her into Mom overdrive. "What happened, honey? Did something happen?"

"No, nothing happened. It was okay, I guess."

"Well," Mom said. "It takes a while to fit in. You'll make new friends soon." She reached over and stroked the back of my neck like she usually does. Normally I like it, but not when parked in front of the whole world.

"Mom!" I ducked down in the seat. "Can we go now, please?"

She'd made plans for us to show Dad the new house we'd found. (Meanwhile we were living in a hotel.) Since Dad had already started his new job, Mom and I were in charge of finding a home to buy. We'd seen about a dozen places before Mr. Garcia, our real estate agent, had shown us this one.

Mom and I really liked the layout and interior detailing—with hallway skylights and granite countertops. I always notice stuff like that. Dad says

I should study in college to become a designer, but I haven't decided yet.

Sometimes at the supermarket I'll get a design magazine and flip through the pages, thinking how I'd do a room with different furniture or colors. I guess I'm weird that way. With my guy friends back home I'd play along with combat video games, but what I really liked was sketching house plans, buildings, and stuff. Maybe that's why I've always been better friends with girls.

When Mom and I arrived in the driveway of the white stucco town house, Dad and Mr. Garcia, a big guy with a thick black mustache, were already waiting.

I led Dad through each room, pointing out where everything should go. "We could put the sofa here . . . and your chair there. It's perfect—and only six blocks from school, so I wouldn't even have to take the bus. Come check out the counter space in the kitchen!"

In our old house Mom always complained that the counter space wasn't enough. I noticed it too, the times when I made everyone breakfast.

I like to cook. My specialty is omelets—mushroom, ham and cheese . . . I like to experiment with different kinds. Usually they turn out really good, except for the disaster I filled with popcorn. Not even Dad would eat it, and he was pretty hungry.

After the kitchen I showed him the den. "This could be Mom's office. Right, Mom?" She's an accountant and sometimes works from home.

Upstairs I'd already picked out my bedroom. On one side a picture window looked over the back patio. Across the room a door opened to a huge closet—great to organize my stuff.

My friend Janice (who Pen Girl reminds me of) says I'm a neat freak. She laughs because I arrange my clothes by color, but it looks really cool.

I hauled Dad to the master bedroom and pressed my finger against the windowpane. "Look, you can see the golf course at the foot of the hill."

I was sure that would win him over. Dad's a total golf fanatic. It's part of the reason when he got laid off he looked for a job someplace warmer. Even though I'm not crazy about golf, sometimes I like to go with him just to be together.

"Dad," I said, looking up at him. "We've got to get this place."

Dad's a lot taller than me—over six feet. Apart from that, people say we look alike. I guess we do.

"All right." He patted me on the shoulder, laughing. "You sold me."

For the next hour Mr. Garcia wrote up a contract and called the seller's agent. I tried doing my homework but I was too wired to concentrate.

"When can we move in?" I asked on the drive to dinner.

Mom explained we'd have to wait for our offer to be accepted. "Hopefully we'll hear by tomorrow."

"Tomorrow?" I groaned, not knowing if I could wait that long.

After we stopped for pizza, I rode with Dad. He asked me about school and gave me a pack of chocolate mints a coworker had given him as a welcome present. Dad's allergic to chocolate, which sucks for him, but it's great for me.

When we got to our tiny hotel suite, he let me use his laptop to get online with my Wisconsin friends. In addition to Janice (screen name: LifeHuggerXXOO), there's Marcie (SN: No_Broccoli_Please). Marcie's the complete opposite of Janice—quiet, brainy, and a really fussy eater. Then there's William (GameBoy353), my best guy friend. He's a total gamer, constantly downloading new ones off the Web.

The four of us always hung out together, and even when apart constantly phoned or instant messaged each other. We also led my school's drama club. Before I left they gave me a mini Oscar statue as a going-away present since I was heading to California. I thought that was pretty funny.

Tonight I IM'd them about my sucky new school

that I found out doesn't even have a drama club. And I told them about the awesome house. They caught me up on stuff back at home. Today marked ten days since the last time I'd seen them. It felt so great to talk I didn't want to log off. But because it's two hours later there, they had to go. The time-change thing really blows.

After finishing my homework I prepared my backpack for school and checked to make sure my pen worked, so I could return Pen Girl's.

A little later Mr. Garcia called to say the seller had accepted our offer on the house. I leaped off the couch, jumping up and down. Dad raised his arm, high-fiving me, and with his other arm hugged Mom. It was after eleven before we all finally calmed down. Dad helped me unfold the sleeping couch.

I climbed beneath the covers thinking about the different ways I might lay out the furniture in my new bedroom. Then I thought about school, dreading lunchtime and sitting by myself. Suddenly I thought of something else.

I got out of bed and put one of the chocolate mints Dad had given me next to Pen Girl's pen in my backpack. Then I climbed back beneath the covers and went to sleep.

# Chapter 3

## Xio

Today in first period Frederick returned my pen—
and gave me a chocolate! Can I, like, just marry him
now, please?

At lunch it killed me to see him sitting by himself
in the nerd section. Not that I have anything against
nerds, but that just wasn't where he belonged.

"We've got to invite Frederick to sit with us," I told
my group.

We call ourselves *Las Sexy Seis* (the Sexy Six)—
even though Carmen's the only one who's had anything remotely close to actual sex. This past summer
she actually showed Victor Carrera (the most *guapo*
hottie at San Cayetano Middle) her boobs!

The rest of us aren't quite so daredevil. That's
probably why we all look up to her, even though
we're about the same age. Carmen's also the
prettiest, with deep, dark eyes and a Barbie doll
figure.

Then there's Nora. She's the brainiest—always studying, a true worker-bee Virgo. We're always trying to pull her away from the books. ("Nora, stop being a bore-a.") But then we rely on her at exam time. She's cute too, but she'd be cuter if she'd ditch the boxy glasses and volumize her hair. We've got to work on that.

Our conscience is María, a.k.a. *Santa María*. To picture her, imagine a tiny Chihuahua with big brown eyes trembling from worry. Whenever someone comes up with a fun idea, she's certain to gasp, *"Ay, Dios mío!* We'd better not."

I suspect she secretly likes us prodding her though, because in the end she always tags along, like a little sister not wanting to get left behind.

Josefina (she goes by José) is the jockiest of us and gets called names a lot—Lesbo, dumb stuff like that. But I always feel safe when I'm with her. She's big for thirteen—nearly six feet tall. Think Warrior Princess, with broad shoulders and boyish hair. She's our defender against any guy who gets too obnoxious, but with friends she's a gentle giant. She's probably the most levelheaded of us too.

The last of our six was Gloria, but she moved away to Nevada last summer. She was always clowning and cracking us up with dumb sex jokes. I miss her.

We've all known each other since grade school.

Even though we're each a little bit different we share a lot. All of our parents are immigrants. None of our real dads live with us—except José's. We all want to do something with our lives—be something. And meanwhile, we have a great time together. There's always someone to IM school gossip or phone for help with homework or just come over and hang out.

And right now we were all staring across the cafeteria at Frederick.

"Why's he sitting in the nerd section?" Carmen said, licking ketchup from her fingers.

"He's new." José put down her burger, speaking up for him. "He probably hasn't made any friends yet."

Nora glanced over her glasses, studying him. "Maybe he's a social misfit."

"Or a psycho!" María's eyes widened.

"He's neither." I said sternly. "I'm going to invite him to sit with us."

"Let's all go sit with him," Carmen suggested. "That way he can't say no. With guys you have to keep the upper hand at all times."

I don't know how Carmen comes up with stuff like that, but it made sense.

"Come on," I agreed, pushing my chair back. "Everyone, let's go!"

"I can't believe we're doing this," María whispered, grabbing her tray to follow us.

Frederick glanced up from his meal as the five of us marched across the lunchroom and surrounded him, trying not to giggle. We didn't succeed much.

"Hi, mind if we sit with you?" I slid my tray onto his table and sat down, introducing everyone. "We're, like, the welcoming committee." (More uncontrollable giggles.)

"You can ask us anything you like," Carmen offered.

"And we have some questions for you." That was Nora, turned private investigator.

We found out he's from a town called Eau Claire, which Nora spelled for us. He's Lutheran, which María said is basically like Catholic, except they don't believe in the pope. José found out he likes sports but gets asthma. And I learned his zodiac sign is Cancer; the same as Papi's. That means he's gentle, sensitive, moody, and a little bit insecure. I like that in a guy.

"Can you speak any Spanish?" Carmen asked, putting on a serious look, which warned me she was up to something.

"Um, not really," Frederick told her. "Just from—you know—restaurants."

*"Ah!"* Carmen grinned. *"Pues, Xio está súper caliente para ti."*

José and Nora burst out laughing, while María blushed. Carmen had just told Frederick I was super hot for him.

"Huh?" Frederick said. "What's that mean?"

I pinched Carmen's arm, totally annoyed, which only provoked her more.

"Do you have a girlfriend?" Carmen asked, in English this time.

"Carmen, you are so nosy!" I pretended to be mad, though underneath I was dying to hear his response.

"No," he said sheepishly. The poor guy had turned red as a chili pepper.

"That's good." Carmen laughed, nudging me.

I'm sure Frederick must've been *so* relieved when the bell rang. He probably thought we were a bunch of kooks.

"Did you want to ask *us* anything?" I said, walking alongside him to the tray return. "We didn't really give you much of a chance."

"Hmn . . ." He glanced down at his tray, his brow knitting, and then looked up at me. "Can I sit with you guys again tomorrow?"

"Sure!" I must've broken into a huge smile. He did too. And I noticed he's not hugely shorter than I am. If he stood on his toes and I bent down an inch, we'd be precisely the same height.

# Chapter 4

## Frederick

Thirty-three days after leaving Wisconsin we finally moved into our new house. I wanted to take the day off from school to help, but Mom wouldn't let me. So I drew a floor plan to show her where I thought the movers should put everything.

My room is awesome. I arranged my desk and computer near the window so I could look out over the patio. And I put my TV across from the bed so I could lie down to watch it. I spent the weekend organizing everything—my CDs, design magazines, and DVDs. It's great to have all my stuff again.

With Dad's digital camera I took about two dozen photos of every room in the house, plus the outside, and e-mailed the pics to everyone back home on my Buddy List.

I'd told everybody about Xio and her friends. Ever since that second day at lunch I sat together with them, hearing stories about family arguments, comments on other girls' makeup, guesses about who has a crush on whom, and opinions about teachers' hairdos (or as Carmen calls them, "hair-*don'ts*").

One night while IMing my friends in Wisconsin, Janice asked: *Have you made any guy friends yet?*

*Not really,* I typed back, a little embarrassed. I'd wanted to make friends with other boys but it hadn't happened as easy as with Xio and her group.

On some afternoons, as I walked home past the grassy field behind school, I had noticed a group of about twenty boys playing soccer—shouting and calling to each other, partly in English, partly in Spanish. "Spanglish," Xio calls it. Most of the guys were bigger than me. But then who my age isn't bigger than me?

Dad always tells me that in order to grow I should get more involved in sports. But Mom freaks out because of my asthma, and they start arguing.

No matter where I go she's always reminding me, "Do you have your inhaler?"

Today as I passed the soccer field I slowed down, watching the boys kick the ball back and forth. At the front of the group a tall boy with wavy black hair took control of the ball, kicking it in front of him.

I remembered him from one time when he stopped by our lunch table and talked to Carmen. I'd wondered if he was her boyfriend.

As the other boys now raced to catch him, he laughed over his shoulder at them. He seemed so . . . how can I describe it? It's like he was the boy I wished I could be—tall, strong, athletic, popular with the other guys. . . .

All of a sudden the soccer ball came flying in my direction, bouncing across the grass. Quickly I jogged over, putting my foot out to stop it. As I picked it up the boys called and shouted for me to send it back.

"Hey, over here!" Tall Boy waved to me.

I kicked the ball toward him—a little high, but no matter. He stopped it with the side of his knee and quickly punted it before any other boys could intercept it. Then he sprinted downfield, trading the ball between himself and his teammates.

As he approached the end line he swung his foot back and slammed the ball. The goalie leaped to block it, but the ball sailed beneath his outstretched arms.

"Goooooal!" Tall Boy and his teammates shouted, jumping up and down, thrusting their arms high in the air.

While the goalie ran to fetch the ball, Tall Boy grabbed his T-shirt sleeve to wipe his face. Then he spotted me, and with a huge grin gave me the thumbs-up. And I gave it back.

\* \* \*

In the hall later that week I saw him talking to Carmen again. Casually I walked up to her and we said hi.

The tall boy looked over at me, cocking his head to one side. Up close I could see he was starting to grow a faint layer of mustache fuzz. Mine hadn't started growing yet.

"You were at the field the other day," he told me.

"Yeah!" I smiled, happy he remembered.

"Yeah," he agreed, grinning back. "What's your name?"

"This is Frederick," Carmen answered for me. "Not Fred. Frederick."

"Hey, I'm Victor." He raised his hand up for me to clasp. His grip was strong but easy. "You should come play with us after school."

My first thought was: *Awesome!* My second thought was: *But what if Mom freaks out because of my asthma?* My third thought was: *Does she have to know?*

The bell rang and Carmen nodded to me. "I'll tell Xio you're playing. We'll all come watch."

Victor clapped me on the shoulder. "See you after school." He gave me the thumbs-up again and I watched him walk away with Carmen.

After the last period bell I headed toward the grassy field. Several boys were kicking the ball between them, warming up. Others peeled off their backpacks as they arrived, tossing them into a cluster. On the aluminum bleachers Xio and her friends called to me, cheering. "Frederick! Frederick! Rah, rah, rah!"

"Hey, Federico!" Victor shouted, waving me over. "Come meet my buds."

I slid off my backpack, dropped it on the pile, and walked over.

"Hey, everyone, this is Federico."

"Hey," some boys said, and others nodded, while others kept kicking the soccer ball.

"You're on my team." Victor grabbed my shoulder. He was a lot more physical than guys in Wisconsin. I'd noticed a lot of the Mexican boys were.

As we ran onto the field to start playing, I suddenly realized I'd left my inhaler in my backpack. Crud.

"Wait a minute!" I shouted and hurried to get it.

Victor watched me stuff the tube into my pocket. "What's that?"

The other boys turned to look.

"Um . . . it's in case I get asthma."

"What if the little guy dies on us?" a boy bouncing the ball said and the others laughed. I hated having asthma.

"Look, it's no big deal," I assured Victor. "As long as I don't get too winded."

Victor rubbed a hand across his chin, giving me a long look. I waited, sweating in the sun and wondering, *Will he tell me I can't play?*

Suddenly his face lit up. "Hey, Gordo!" he shouted to a heavyset guy guarding the goal box. "Let Rico play goalie."

"Sure!" Gordo said, and happily trotted toward us.

In one awesome stroke Victor had resolved my whole dilemma. He'd also abbreviated my name. And yet for some reason it didn't bother me. But that didn't mean I'd let anyone else do it.

As the other boys raced up and down the field, I hunkered down, protecting our goal box. Only once in a while did I have to dive to stop a ball. Each time I succeeded, Xio and her friends leaped into the air, making up goofy cheers.

Halfway through the game one of the boys twisted his ankle and had to step out. José ran in to substitute and played better than most of the guys.

By the end of the game I'd blocked five goals without missing a single one.

Victor panted over to me, his skin shiny with sweat. "Hey, you're pretty good, Rico." He patted my shoulder again. I was starting to get used to it.

"You were *fabuloso!*" Xio said, running over to join us.

At dinner, I wanted so badly to tell Mom and Dad about playing soccer with my new friend Victor. But what if Mom went ballistic? Instead I IM'd my Wisconsin friends about it after dinner.

The first thing Janice asked was: *Is Victor cute?*

I stared at the screen, debating how to answer.

Often when I was with girls they commented stuff about guys, like: "Total hottie" or "He's *so* yummy."

If I thought the guy was a jerk, I'd argue, "No way! Yuck! He's gross!"

But if I agreed a boy was cute I'd never say it aloud. Although it's okay for girls to say other girls are cute, everyone knows guys can't say stuff like that about other guys. I'd made that mistake once in fourth grade—and got called gay for a month afterward. That's so stupid because guys know which guys are good-looking and which aren't. Why should saying it out loud mean you're gay?

Even so, I only typed to Janice: *You'd probably like him.*

We continued IMing between homework assignments till everyone had to log off. Then I put my books away and lay on the carpet—listening to CDs, and thinking about Victor.

# Chapter 5

## Xio

While I helped Mami make burgers for dinner I told her about Frederick playing soccer and I showed Stevie the cheers my friends and I had made up, such as: "Not just Fred! Not just Rick! Iiiiit's Frederick!"

"Very nice," Mami said. "Come to the table."

"*Ay,* Mami, he's so cute! His eyes are bluer than the ocean. And his skin is whiter than this milk." I lifted my glass. "And his smile is like . . . like . . . sunshine."

I told her how in the weeks I'd known him he'd brought me chocolate mints and printed out a beautiful map of Europe for my social studies project. ". . . And he's such a good listener!"

"That's good," Mami said, and gave a soft laugh. She's not a big laugher like me. She's more subdued in everything—how she talks and dresses. I'm always trying to get her to wear more makeup—and she's always telling me to wear less.

After dinner, while I helped clean up, the phone rang. "I'll get it!" I jumped for the receiver. "Hello?"

"Hello," answered a man's voice.

For an instant, my heart rocketed against my chest. Was it Papi?

"Is your mom there?" the man continued.

My heart crashed back to earth. No, it wasn't Papi.

"Who's calling?" I asked politely, dying to know.

"Rodolfo." The name trilled off his tongue.

I covered the mouthpiece and whispered to Mami, "Who's Rodolfo?"

Her eyes brightened instantly. Real pronto, she dried her hands on the dishcloth and patted her hair. Did she think he could see her through the phone?

"Mami, who is he?" I insisted, but she'd already grabbed the receiver.

"Hello?" she said softly. Then she smiled and turned away, blushing.

*Hmn,* I thought. Was Mami going to start dating again? After the last guy, a car salesman who it turned out wasn't even divorced yet, Mami had said she wasn't going to date anymore. But judging from her smile, was she reconsidering?

I hoped so. Although some of my friends didn't like their moms to date, I worried my mom was letting her heart grow hard and cold and closed. A

million times I'd told her, "It's not good for someone
your age to be single." After all, she was thirty-six
already. And besides . . . if she was dating then maybe
she wouldn't be so overprotective about me dating—
which I hoped I'd begin soon.

While Mami talked on the phone with the Rodolfo
guy, I finished rinsing dinner plates and loaded the
dishwasher gently, so I wouldn't disturb her. And so I
could hear.

"Yes, that was my daughter," Mami was saying. "I
also have a son who's six. Do you have any
children?"

As she listened she wiped the counter with a
sponge, moving the sugar and salt canisters back and
forth.

"In college?" Mami asked into the phone. "That's
nice."

They talked about all sorts of stuff—work (Mami's
a sales manager), Guadalajara (where she's from),
and about how proud she is of Stevie and me.

From Mami's side of the conversation, I gathered
Mr. Rodolfo was widowed and had a daughter. And
apparently . . . was he asking Mami for a date?

"This weekend?" Mami said, sponging the cleaned
counter again.

He *was* asking her for a date. "Say yes!" I
whispered. "Go out with him!"

Mami flashed her eyes at me and turned away. "I'm not ready to rush into anything," she said into the phone. "But I've enjoyed your call tonight. I'd like to talk again another evening. Would that be all right? Great. Thanks for calling. *Buenas noches.*"

"Mami!" I exclaimed as soon as she hung up. "Don't you like him? Who is he?"

"We met at that company dinner last week." Mami put down the sponge. "He's very nice but I'm not ready for a date yet. I want to get to know him better first."

"Mami! You already know he's nice. Why won't you go out with him?"

*"Ay, mi hija . . ."* She began wiping the counter again for the millionth time.

I couldn't believe her. "When *I* get to be an adult, if I want to go out with a guy who calls me, I'm not waiting." I closed the dishwasher. "Were you this way with Papi?"

"No." She put down the sponge and crossed her arms. "With him I went out the night after we met."

She'd told me a lot of the story before—how they met through friends and she fell head over heels at first sight.

"That's why I want to go more slowly now." She reached out to stroke my hair. "Let's make a deal. I'll worry about my love life, and you worry about yours. Okay?"

"*What* love life?" I groaned.

Watching IMs from Frederick (SketcherDude54701) pop up on my computer screen was hardly my idea of passion—although I was still thrilled about it.

Even better, I loved listening to his voice on the phone. It's going through that changing thing boys go through, where it cracks every so often. I think that's so sexy.

The first couple of times I called him he stuttered *um*s and cleared his throat the entire time. But now he and I talk about everything—school, his friends in Wisconsin, our favorite colors. Mine's bright yellow, the color of the sun. His is teal, which I'd never heard of. He said it's a greenish blue. His favorite food is pizza, same as mine. We both enjoy the same music. (Like most boys, he claims he's not crazy about boy bands, but he seems to know them all.) We have so much in common it's amazing.

Like when I asked him, "If you could have a talk with any famous person in history, who would it be?"

He told me to go first and I said, "Mother Theresa. I think she was awesome, the way she gave up everything to help needy people."

And Frederick said his person would be Gandhi. "He was brave but never violent."

Isn't it incredible that both our people knew each other in India? I think.

Then I asked, "If you died and became a ghost, where would you haunt?"

He said his old home in Wisconsin. It sounded like he still missed it.

I said my grandparents' house in Guadalajara, which is my favorite place on earth.

Tonight Frederick and I talked for more than an hour till his dad needed to use the phone. I tried to recall Mami's words when she hung up with Rodolfo.

"I enjoyed talking with you tonight."

"Huh?" Frederick replied. "Oh yeah. Me too."

*"Buenas noches,"* I said softly.

He tried to say it back, but it sounded like *Bonus new cheese.*

After hanging up I snuggled between the pillows on my bed. I have about a thousand. Except I imagined it was Frederick beside me instead of pillows. And I imagined taking his hand in mine.

*What kind of movies does he like?* I wondered. Maybe we could go sometime. Mami could go as slow as she wanted, but I wasn't waiting around.

# Chapter 6

## Frederick

Xio was becoming my best friend. Ever since she'd first phoned me we talked almost every night. Actually she did most of the talking, but I liked listening to her.

She told me all kinds of stuff—about her girlfriends, mom, and little brother. She said she was mad at her dad because he didn't call on her birthday. Even though she said she didn't care about him anymore, I thought she did.

She also asked me all sorts of questions—some interesting ones, like: "Do you ever wish you had a brother or sister?"

"Yeah, sometimes," I told her. "When I'm lonely or mad at my parents."

Other times her questions were really weird, like: "Have you ever wished you were a girl?"

"Um, no. I like being a guy. Why would I want to be a girl?"

"I don't know." She giggled. "Just to try it."

Sometimes while Xio and I were on the phone and doing homework, I also IM'd my friends in Wisconsin.

One night Marcie told me it had been fifty days since I'd left. Wow. That long? I'd stopped keeping track. I no longer thought about Marcie and Janice and William all the time. And I didn't race home at the end of the day to check my e-mail.

Lots of days I played soccer after school. The pickup games never really started until Victor showed up. I'd drop my backpack onto the pile and gaze along with the other boys toward the school door, waiting.

Even across the distance I recognized Victor's smile the instant he popped out of the building. His long legs bounded across the field in steps as big as I could jump, while boys on each side of him joked and play punched.

Walking closer, he tossed his backpack, adding it to the pile. Then he stripped off his top shirt, revealing his white T-shirted chest as he started assigning boys to teams.

All of us looked up to Victor, as if he were our coach—not because he was tallest or fastest or strongest or best, although he was all those things. It was more than that. It was as if there was something radiating from his smile and cheering voice that made us all want to be with him.

Maybe that's why it didn't bother me that he called me Rico. But I still wouldn't let anybody else do it, not even Xio.

Victor clapped once for the game to begin. And as he ran past me onto the field, his breeze brushed my skin, making it tingle.

For the next hour I'd stand at my goal box, watching him run, kick, or bounce the ball off his head. I didn't know why watching him made me smile so much, but by the end of the game my cheek muscles always hurt.

His tanned arms turned shiny with sweat, and I noticed the soft fuzz above his lip collect a string of droplets that looked like tiny diamonds.

"How you doing, Rico?" he asked when we finally headed off the field.

"I'm doing good," I told him. He swung his arm around my shoulder and we joked awhile, then I headed home.

Mom had been interviewing for jobs with accounting firms and meantime worked on the accounts of people back in Wisconsin. She was sitting at her computer one day when I arrived from soccer.

*"Hola,"* I said. (Xio had taught me how to say hello in Spanish.)

*"Hola* to you too," Mom said in a stern voice. "Where were you? I was starting to worry." She gave the air a little sniff. "Have you been sweating?"

Uh-oh. Beneath her gaze I started sweating again—big time. I hadn't told her and Dad about playing soccer yet.

"Um . . . I was just at school, hanging out with friends. I'll go take a shower."

Before she could say anything I hurried upstairs.

While soaping up I decided I'd better tell her the truth—before she went bonkers thinking I was doing drugs or robbing banks. Except . . . maybe I should tell Dad first. After all, he'd encouraged me to get involved in sports.

After dinner I pretended to need help with science, asking Dad, "Can you help me with some essay questions?"

Since Dad works in science (he's a chemical engineer), his face always lights up when I ask him for help with it. In my room we reviewed the essay questions.

"Ohhh, I get it now. Thanks, Dad. By the way, can I, um, talk to you about something?" I took a deep breath.

As I told him about soccer he got the disappointed

scowl he gets when I do something wrong.

"You shouldn't keep stuff like this from your mom and me."

"I know. But what if Mom doesn't want me to play? She's always worrying. She won't let me do anything! You said I need to do sports to grow."

Dad's frown softened as he scratched a hand across his chest, like he does when he's mulling something over.

"Well," he said at last. "Let's you and me go talk to her."

I got a feeling from the way he said it that he was on my side.

"That was fast." Mom glanced up from the newspaper.

I sat down on the couch and looked to Dad. He nodded, encouraging me.

"Mom . . . can I talk to you about something?"

Her eyes darted between me and Dad. "Is something the matter?"

Crud. She was already freaking out. I took a big gulp of air and told her about soccer.

"Honey!" she quickly folded her paper. "Something could've happened to you!"

"Nothing happened, Mom. I play goalie. It's like waiting for a bus."

Of course, it's not really like that. Some days I'm

running constantly to block one ball after another. But I didn't tell Mom that.

"Well, he needs to get some exercise," Dad said. "And playing goalie is probably the least strenuous thing he could do."

Mom glared across the living room at him, and I thought for sure they'd start arguing. But then she turned to me. "How often do you play?"

"Only when enough guys show up. Not every day."

Mom exhaled a huge sigh. "All right. But make sure you carry your inhaler with you. Promise?"

"I promise," I said, and Dad winked at me, smiling.

I bounded upstairs and called Xio to tell her everything that had happened.

"Wow," she said. "I didn't know asthma was so serious. Maybe you shouldn't play."

Oh, great. Now *she* was worried. Are all females like that?

At lunch the following day, Carmen was trying to get me to say dirty words in Spanish by not telling me what I was saying till after I'd said it. She'd done that a few times over the past few weeks till I started catching on.

"I'm not going to repeat that," I told her.

"Good for you!" María cheered me on.

"Here comes Iggy!" Nora interrupted.

I followed her gaze across the lunchroom to the Mexican boy I'd noticed in the hall my first day—the one who smiled like he knew me. Dimple Guy.

"You mean *icky*," Carmen murmured, making a sour face. "I think *maricónes* are so gross."

"*En serio?*" María put down her yogurt. "You really think he's a gay?"

I recalled the boys picking on him, but I knew that calling someone gay didn't mean they actually were gay. It was simply a put-down, like: "That's so gay. He's so gay. Those French fries are so gay." Everyone said it all the time.

"*Ay, por favor*," Carmen insisted. "He's so obvious. Look at how bouncy he walks. Listen to how he says his esses. And those dimples make him look cute as a girl."

I observed him walking toward us. I didn't think he walked so weird.

"Carmen," José whispered. "Just because a cute boy isn't hot for you doesn't mean he's gay."

"Shh!" Xio said. "Be nice. Here he comes."

"*Hola*, Iggy," the girls sang out, smiling sweet as could be—even Carmen.

"Hi," he said, grinning at everyone, his gaze landing on me. Quickly I glanced away. What if it was true what Carmen had said? Was that why he'd smiled at me the first day—and now? Did he think *I* was gay?

While Iggy talked to the girls, I gazed down at my tray and listened to his esses. I guess they sounded a little whistley. What did mine sound like?

After a few minutes Iggy started to say bye to the girls. I glanced up and he looked over at me. "My name's Iggy."

"Hi, um, I'm Frederick." My face grew warm from embarrassment. But why was I embarrassed?

He smiled and told everyone, "See you," and the girls all said, "Bye."

As he stepped away Carmen gave me a huge grin, announcing in a singsong voice, "I think he likes you!"

I glared at her, trying to think what to respond. "You're crazy," I said lamely.

"And you're blushing," Nora told me from behind her glasses. The other girls giggled, except for Xio.

"Would you all grow up?" she said. To my relief, after that she changed the subject to some new video she'd seen on MTV en Español.

Later that week I was at my locker when I spotted Iggy across the crowded hall. Some boys—including Victor and a couple of the soccer guys were laughing and making fun of him. This time I recognized what they were saying, using the same word Carmen had used: *Maricón.* I figured it meant something like "fag" or "queer."

I stood watching, silent. I wanted to tell the guys to stop picking on him. But what could I say? What if the guys started calling me names? What if they didn't want me to play soccer with them anymore? What if they thought *I* was gay?

That afternoon I didn't feel like playing soccer. Instead I walked home, wishing I'd never left Wisconsin.

# Chapter 7

## Xio

*Gracias a Dios!* After three more phone calls Mami *finally* agreed to go on a date with Rodolfo—her first date in more than a year.

While she showered to get ready I lay on top of her bed, flipping through her *Latina* magazine.

"Mami!" I shouted as soon as the water turned off. "What are you wearing tonight?"

"The gray plaid suit!" she yelled from the bathroom.

What? No way! I tossed down the magazine, rushed to the bathroom, tapped on the door, and opened it. "Mami, you can't wear a *pantsuit* on a date."

She stood in her terry cloth robe, plugging in the blow-dryer. "*Cielito,* it'll be fine."

"Mami, no!" I pleaded. "You'll make him yawn to death. I'll pick out something really pretty for you. You'll see."

I quickly closed the door again and while Mami blew-dry her hair, I buried the coma-inducing gray suit in the farthest corner of her closet. In its place I brought out a burgundy beaded skirt that makes Mami shimmer as she walks. I know all her clothes.

For her top I selected a sleeveless silk blouse with a low-cut front. It totally highlights Mami's curves. She's got great cleavage for her age. Plus, the blouse has a matching wrap—excellent for covering (or revealing) shoulders. *Very* strategic.

Mami emerged from the bathroom and scanned the outfit I'd spread on the bed. Her brow crinkled at the black lace bra and panties. "And why these? He's not going to see my underclothes."

"But they'll make you *feel* sexy."

"*Ay, mi hijita.*" Mami rolled her eyes. "How did you grow up so fast?"

While she sat at her vanity, I helped her pick out some dark, shimmery eye shadow and a rosy gloss to give her lips more bite.

"It's all about shimmer," I kept telling her as I brushed her hair.

At exactly seven o'clock the doorbell rang, just as Mami was zipping up her skirt. "Can you get it, *cariño*? Tell him I'll be right out."

"Don't forget the ankle-wrap heels!" I yelled and ran to the front hallway, dying to see Mami's date.

When I swung open the front door, I swear my breath escaped me. The man could've been a movie star—tall, dark, with a trim mustache and dazzling green eyes.

"You must be Xio." His voice was deep and gentle. "I'm Rodolfo."

"Um . . ." I nodded, breathless. "I'll get her." I spun around, then stopped. I turned back. "Oops, sorry. Come in."

He stepped inside, carrying a gold cardboard box I recognized as really expensive chocolates. I knew right then he had potential for making an excellent stepdad.

"Um, have a seat," I said, leading him to the living room. Then I hurried to Mami's room and softly closed the door. "*Ay,* Mami!" I leaned against the door to catch my breath. "He's really, really handsome."

"You think so?" Mami smiled as she dabbed perfume onto her wrists and rubbed them together.

"Big time!" I walked over and reached my hands under her hair, spreading it so it flowed over her shoulders. She looked totally *guapa* in the outfit I'd chosen.

Rodolfo thought so too, telling her how beautiful she looked while my pain-in-the-butt little brother peppered him with questions: "What kind of car is that? Do you have a dog? Where you going? Can I go?"

I'd agreed to stay home with him, and fixed us tacos since they're easy to make. (I'm not big on cooking.) Along with dinner, I conference-called the Sexies to tell them about Mami's drop-dead gorgeous date.

Even though I was supposed to make Stevie go to bed by ten, I let him stay up with me to watch a movie. At a little before eleven, a car pulled into the driveway. I jumped up, tiptoed to the front window, and peeked out the curtain.

"Let me see!" Stevie whispered as he crowded in beside me.

I put a finger to my lips, shushing him. We peered outside, watching Rodolfo open the car door for Mami. As he followed her up the walkway, I couldn't hear what they said but their voices sounded happy.

At the doorstep Mami gave a soft laugh, and slowly Rodolfo leaned over.

"They're kissing!" Stevie clutched hold of my pant leg.

I realized he'd never seen Mami kiss a man, not this way. Stevie had been too small when Papi left. And this was a *long* kiss. Only after Rodolfo pulled away did I notice I'd been holding my breath.

As if tipping a hat goodnight, Rodolfo tapped his forehead with his fingertips.

*"Buenas noches!"* Mami called, watching him walk to his car. Then she turned toward our door.

"Quick!" I nudged Stevie. He and I scrambled across the room. "And don't you dare say we saw them!"

Mami opened the door to see us sitting side by side on the sofa, quietly watching TV, the perfect brother and sis.

"Hi, Mami! You have a nice time?"

*"Very* nice." She tossed her keys onto the hall table and walked toward the sofa.

Stevie and I scooted apart so she could sit between us, and I helped her unstrap her shoes.

"And why isn't Mr. Stevie in bed?" Mami tried to sound cross though she was smiling.

"Because this is a special night for you," I replied. How could she argue with that? "Tell us about your date."

She laughed, draping her arms around our shoulders, and described the fancy restaurant Rodolfo had taken her to and how afterward they strolled alongside the marina.

As she spoke Stevie glanced across her lap at me, his cheeks bulging from stifled giggles. But I gave him the meanest look I could so he'd keep quiet.

After Mami put him to bed, I reminded her about Rodolfo's golden box of chocolates. "Notice, I didn't open it," I said proudly, and we each had a couple. Delicious!

Seeing Mami so happy made me hugely aware that two whole months of eighth grade had gone by— and where was *my* dream date?

Sunday afternoon I called a meeting of the Sexies at my house.

"This is hideously, horribly wrong," I told them. "I'm the only teenage girl in all of San Cayetano who doesn't have a boyfriend."

"Hey, I don't either," Nora corrected.

"Me neither!" José shouted.

"*Yo tampoco,*" María chimed in.

They lay on the carpet, huddled around a fashion magazine Carmen had brought over, checking out what was new, who was hot, and what celebrity was involved with whom, while I paced the room chewing the ends of my hair.

"Why don't you invite Frederick to a movie?" Carmen asked, pulling a bottle of silver sparkle polish from her bag.

"I already thought of that. But he's the guy. He should be calling me. Do I have to do everything?"

While talking I leaned over Nora's shoulder and looked at a photo of a thin blonde starlet. Then I glanced in the mirror at my own body. It seemed to be changing every day. My legs and hips were losing their boniness, which was a good thing. I was finally developing the *curvas* a girl's body is supposed to have. But what if the curves kept growing till I was a full-size blimp?

"Do you think my butt's growing too big?" I asked.

"Your butt's fine," Nora assured me. "If you want, *I'll* tell Frederick to invite you to the movie."

"Don't you dare!" I spun around from the mirror. "That would be *so* elementary school. Besides . . . what if he only likes me as a friend?"

"Then he's gay," Carmen said, brushing polish onto her nails.

"You've got gay on the brain." José scowled at her.

"Well, I think he likes you a lot," María told me, then abruptly turned to the magazine. *"Ay, Dios mío!* Look at how low this guy's wearing his pants."

Like trained dogs we all leaped to look at the photo.

Carmen was the first to lean back again. "Stop worrying about Frederick. Of course he'll want to be more than friends. He's a boy, isn't he? I don't care how *inocente* he looks—boys only want one thing." She made a gesture with her hands.

*"Ay,* Carmen, don't do that." María blushed.

"Why don't we all go to the movie together?" Nora suggested.

"Let's see that Halloween one!" José sat up excitedly.

"Where the chick gets obsessed with the jock? And when he dumps her she tries to slash him to death?"

María shuddered. "That sounds creepy."

"It sounds lame." Nora yawned.

It didn't exactly sound like a date movie to me—unless your date was a serial killer. "That's supposed to make Frederick feel romantic?"

"Fright flicks are the best excuse for holding hands." Carmen blew on her nails to dry them.

"Yeah!" Nora laughed. "He'll be scared otherwise you'll slash him."

Monday at lunchtime I stared at my pizza, unable to eat as I psyched myself up to invite Frederick. But why was I so nervous? Wasn't he sure to say yes? After all, he was my friend. Yeah, but did he want to be *more* than that?

"Here he comes!" María whispered.

My heart thumped against my chest as Frederick sat down next to me, saying, "Hi."

I forced a nervous smile. "Hi."

Everyone else turned quiet, waiting for me. Beneath the table, Carmen nudged my leg. After glaring at her I turned to Frederick. "You want to go to the movies with us Saturday?"

"Huh?" He glanced up from his French fries. "A movie?"

The five of us stared at him, nodding.

"Victor's going too," Carmen said.

"Sounds great." Frederick chomped into a French fry.

"You'll go?" I asked, just to be sure.

"Duh!" Carmen said, but it didn't bother me. All I could think was: *He actually said yes!* Of course, I'd known he would. Beats me why I'd been so stressed.

That night for dinner Mami ordered Chinese food, and I told her my movie plans.

"Frederick . . . the new boy?" She passed me the rice. "I'd like to meet him first."

"Mami!" I put down the steaming bowl of rice. "Why are you treating me like a kid?"

Up till then I'd wanted her to meet Frederick, so she could see how cute and smart and funny he was, but why was she making it a condition of going out with him? Was she afraid he might be an ax murderer or something? She'd never insisted on meeting my other friends. Granted, she'd known them since we were little.

"I'm over thirteen years old. Don't you trust me?"

"*Mi amor,* I do trust you. I just want to know your friends. How about if I drive you to the movie and say hi, then I'll leave you alone. Okay?"

"Oh, great. I'll look like a baby in front of everyone." I jabbed my thumb into my mouth and said in a squeaky baby voice, "My mama wants to meet you."

Stevie hooted with laughter. Mami lifted her gaze heavenward and pressed her lips together, trying to keep from laughing.

"It's not funny!" I told them, trying my hardest to keep from laughing too. But why'd she have to be so overprotective?

# Chapter 8

## Frederick

In Wisconsin going to movies with friends was no big deal, but because this would be my first time here, I couldn't stop thinking about it. I was so nervous that I spent all day Saturday trying to decide what to wear.

I chose jeans because I didn't want to be the only one wearing shorts. For my shirt I layered an unbuttoned blue-green plaid over my teal long-sleeve T. For shoes I chose my black sneakers. Last, I put on a puka shell necklace Mom had given me my last birthday.

"Can I borrow some cologne?" I asked Dad. I'd noticed a lot of the Mexican boys wore cologne, even to school.

"Sure." Dad smiled from his bed. He was watching a golf game on TV, while beside him Mom read a gardening magazine. "But just use a little," he told me. "On my first date I slathered on so much, my girl nearly fainted."

"Dad," I said. "This isn't a date. It's a group of us going."

"Oh, right." He glanced at Mom and back at me. "Sorry."

They drove me to the mall and pulled up outside the movie multiplex, where Xio and her friends were waiting. "That's Xio." I pointed her out.

"Xio!" I hollered out the window.

"She's very pretty." Mom smiled over her shoulder to me. "What beautiful hair!"

"Hi!" Xio said, hurrying over to us. "This is my mom." She gestured to a woman in jeans and wedge sandals beside her.

"Hi, we're Frederick's parents." My mom leaned out the car window, shaking hands with Xio's mom, as I hopped out of the car and said hi too.

Carmen, José, and María had walked over and I also introduced them. Xio told me Nora had to baby-sit and couldn't come.

"What about Victor?" I asked.

"He'd better come," Carmen said, checking her watch.

We left Xio's mom talking to my parents while we went inside to the ticket line. Carmen kept searching the crowds for Victor till María finally called out, "There he is!"

He swaggered up just as we got to the ticket

counter. Carmen rattled Spanish at him, angry he was late, but he bought her ticket and she calmed down. Then he turned to me.

"How you doing, Rico?" He held his hand up for me to shake, but then he swung his arm around my shoulder, pulling me into a headlock like he did with his other buddies.

I was only as tall as Victor's shoulders, so my face squished up against his chest. He had a lot more muscles than me, that was for sure. His cologne smelled sweet and good, kind of like brown sugar.

"Hey, cool necklace," he told me, letting me go with a clap on the back.

"Thanks," I said. We all got drinks and stuff. I bought Xio popcorn with the money Mom had given me.

"Let's sit in back," Carmen told us as we shuffled into the movie theater. We scooted single file into the last row, María and José going first.

I'd been hoping to sit with Victor, but Carmen wanted to sit beside him and Xio wanted to sit next to her and also to me. So I sat on the end, munching popcorn and leaning forward so I wouldn't be left out.

"Hey, Rico!" Victor yelled across Carmen and Xio. "You know what you call popcorn in Spanish?"

"Uh-uh. Popcorn-o?"

"Naw." He laughed. "*Palomitas*. Little pigeons. Because they fly!" He pelted a kernel at me.

I ducked. The kernel bounced off my armrest. In retaliation I plucked a kernel from my own bag and chucked it at him.

But instead of dodging my volley, Victor snapped my kernel into his mouth and chomped down with a grin.

"What are you," José asked, "a trained seal?"

"Yeah." Victor started flapping his hands like flippers. "Argh-argh-argh!"

Carmen dug into her own popcorn bag and tossed a handful at him, followed by Xio and me, all of us laughing.

"Hey, ambush!" Victor howled, flinging kernels back at us. "No fair!"

"Guys?" María pleaded. "You're going to get us kicked out."

"Okay, truce." Xio held up her hands. "Previews are starting."

We all sat back in our seats, brushing kernels off us. As the lights dimmed Xio whispered to me, "I like your cologne."

"Huh? Oh yeah. Thanks."

The previews were for one blow-up/shoot-'em-up movie after another. They looked boring to me but with each explosion Victor cheered stuff like: "Kick his butt! Yeah! Sweet!"

The girls tittered and shushed him.

Finally the movie opened with creepy thriller music, cracking thunder, and raging lightning. A teenage guy lay in bed, supposedly managing to sleep during all the noise. Behind him a shadowy figure crept across the room, knife in hand.

Just as the sleeping boy's eyes twitched open, the blade plunged through the air. The boy screamed. And I jumped in my seat.

Beside me Xio giggled.

I slunk down, embarrassed, as the movie hero woke from what turned out to have been only a nightmare.

I leaned back and looked toward Victor, hoping at least he hadn't noticed me jump like a wuss.

But from the looks of it Victor had been too busy to notice. Two seats away, he was sliding his arm around Carmen. I recalled how he'd swung his arm around me in the lobby, except I knew he wasn't going to pull Carmen into a headlock.

His arm embraced her shoulder and she leaned into him. A moment later Victor spotted me watching them and flashed me a grin.

I smiled bashfully back and returned to the movie. Just then Xio gently bumped my hand on the armrest. Figuring she wanted more room, I shifted my hand.

But Xio's hand once again pressed mine. This time I decided to ignore it and watch the film.

The teen hero was now walking down his school hallway, trying to stay loyal to his pink-sweatered sweetheart while a sexy new girl stared at him from her locker, dabbing gloss onto her lips.

Suddenly Xio's hand began creeping on top of mine.

My heart skipped a beat. I glanced down. Xio had grabbed hold of my hand. But why? Was she worried about me because I'd jumped earlier? Maybe I should tell her I was okay. Or was she scared? Or . . . Uh-oh. Had Dad been right? Was this supposed to be a date?

Just then Xio turned my hand over, gently wedging her soft fingers between mine.

I'd never held a girl's hand before—except during field trips when I was little. Never in a romantic way.

Sweat began beading on my forehead. On-screen, the hero's best friend was found covered in blood, slashed to death.

As if that wasn't enough, Xio's thumb began rubbing back and forth across mine. What did that mean? Was it a cue for something? What was I supposed to do?

Victor would know!

I glanced toward him, hoping he might turn from

the movie and somehow signal me advice. But he wasn't exactly watching the movie. In the soft glow of the screen light, he leaned across Carmen—his head bobbing and swaying—as they made out.

I stared, even though I knew I shouldn't. But I couldn't pull myself away. Something stirred inside my chest. *What does it feel like?* I wondered. *What does it taste like? Can she feel the soft fuzz above his lip?*

A prickling below my wrist interrupted my thoughts. It felt as if a thousand tiny ants were crawling over the hand Xio was holding. I looked down just as the tingling stopped. In fact, I no longer felt anything. My hand had fallen dead asleep.

Oh, great. Now what? I knew I should move it to get the blood flowing. Thinking I'd better tell Xio, I turned to her.

She was gazing at the movie, smiling happily. Crud. How could I tell her she'd put my hand to sleep? I didn't want to hurt her feelings.

But what if the lack of circulation caused gangrene or something? Wouldn't Xio feel even worse if I ended up having to get my hand amputated—all because of her?

Nevertheless I couldn't bring myself to say anything. I let my hand stay where it was, my fingers slowly strangling to death, while on-screen the boy's classmates got slashed one by one.

Finally, the movie ended the way it began, except the shadowy figure wielding the knife turned out to be the boy's girlfriend—actually a psycho. Yeah, right—whatever.

"See, Rico?" Victor grinned in the lobby afterward. "You've got to be careful with girls."

I felt myself blush, thinking he'd somehow found out about my hand. But then Carmen made a slashing gesture at him and he jumped behind me, shielding himself and laughing.

We all joked around till José's dad arrived in a minivan and we piled inside. José sat in front, Victor and Carmen in back. Xio, María, and I squeezed into the middle row. I tried not to squish Xio but she said, "That's okay. I don't mind."

As it turned out, I was the first one dropped off at home. I stepped out of the van, feeling sad to tell everyone good night. In spite of the fact I'd risked losing an important appendage, it had been a great evening.

I stood on the walkway, watching the taillights disappear down the moonlit street. The night breeze brushed across my skin and again I saw in my mind Victor kissing.

# Chapter 9

## Xio

As José's dad drove away from Frederick's, I waved through the minivan's window, even though I knew Frederick couldn't see me.

"You're so lucky," María told me. "He's so polite, so sweet. He's perfect."

I cupped my hand around her left ear and whispered, "He held my hand."

"Hey, no secrets!" Victor complained from the back row.

"Xio held hands with Frederick!" Carmen announced to the entire van.

"You did?" José asked from the front seat. "Way to go, Xio!"

"Whoa!" Victor exclaimed. "You got the hots for li'l Rico? I didn't know that."

"Don't you dare say anything to him!" I spun around in my seat. "Carmen, make him promise!"

"Don't you think," Carmen asked, "Frederick's already figured it out?"

"Yeah, but I don't want him to think I'm blabbing it to the whole world."

When I got home Mami was sitting on the sofa watching TV. Stevie lay sprawled across her lap, snoring like a piglet. How could so much racket come from such a little guy? I hoped Frederick didn't snore like that.

Mami lifted the remote and turned down the volume. "Did you have a good time?"

*"Maravilloso! Fantastico! Glorioso!"* I plopped down and took Mami's hand in mine. Frederick's had definitely felt meatier. But Mami's palm felt smoother and drier than Frederick's. His had been damp as a swamp—from nerves, I guess.

*"Cariño?"* Mami wiggled her fingers. "What are you up to?"

"Comparing," I told her as I examined her long, bony fingers.

"He seems like a nice boy," Mami said, leaning against my shoulder.

"Yeah." I sighed. "I told you he was."

On Monday during lunch I made a point of sitting directly beside Frederick and kept my hand in my lap, just in case he wanted to hold it again. But he didn't. Although I liked his being shy, sometimes I wished he wasn't.

I was in a pretty crabby mood for the rest of the afternoon.

Then I got home and found a package on our doorstep. My heart started racing when I saw it was from Papi, addressed to me.

Dying to find out what was inside, I quickly carried the brown cardboard box into the kitchen and set it on the table. But then I thought: *Why should I even care?*

I poured a glass of milk and drank it, staring at the carton. I was still mad at Papi, even though he'd finally phoned a few weeks ago, one night when I was out. He'd told Mami some lame excuse about how he'd been moving the weekend of my birthday, blah, blah, blah. . . .

Mami had left his new number beneath a fridge magnet, but I still hadn't called him. Was I being too harsh?

Unable to fight my curiosity any longer, I tore open the box. Inside were about a hundred foil-wrapped chocolate kisses.

At least he'd remembered my love for chocolate. I unwrapped one, popped it into my mouth, and noticed something pink glimmering beneath the foil wrappings.

I dug my fingers in, tugging at the plastic.

My heart sank. No, it couldn't be . . . a Barbie? Was he joking? I'm over thirteen already!

Wedged between the stupid doll's perfectly trim arms was a note.

> *Dear Xio,*
> *Sorry I couldn't call on your birthday. I hope you*
> *had a good time. Did Mami give you my new phone*
> *number? Call me soon.*
> *Happy birthday!*
> *Many besos, Papi*

I threw down the note, unwrapped another kiss, and chomped down on it. No way was I going to call him. I picked up the doll and stared in amazement.

"I'm not a little girl anymore! Maybe if you'd stuck around you'd know that."

I hurled the Barbie across the room. It hit the wall with a hard *smack!* Then it bounced to the floor.

I unwrapped another chocolate and popped it into my mouth, trying to calm down. The doll sprawled upside down, arms at different angles, head twisted, one foot bare.

I felt kind of sorry for her. I know that's stupid, but it wasn't her fault Papi's a jerk.

I got up, searched for the missing shoe, and found it beside the fridge. I wedged it back onto the tiny foot and brought the doll back to the table.

Brushing her hair back into place, I remembered how Papi used to call me his *Sirenita* (Little Mermaid) because of my own long, thick hair.

Why had he left? Why couldn't he have stayed? Would he ever come back?

I kept eating those stupid kisses all afternoon. By the time Mami brought Stevie home from day care, I was holding my stomach it hurt so much.

Mami pressed her palm on my forehead. "Why did you eat so many?"

"Can I have some?" Stevie begged, his eyes wide as saucers.

"Have all you want," I moaned, but Mami told him, "*Papito,* take only two. You don't want to get sick like your sister."

"He thinks I'm still seven years old," I complained, and Mami understood I meant Papi.

"Call him and tell him you're not. It seems like he's trying to make up."

"I don't want to make up," I groaned, though I wondered: *Why don't I?*

Dads could be so confusing—a favorite late-night discussion topic during Sexies sleepovers.

Among us, the only one whose dad and mom were still together was José. She and her dad were really close—always going to soccer and baseball games together. Maybe that's why she was such a tomboy.

On the other end of the scale, Carmen never even knew her real dad. He left before she was born.

"Heck if I care," was Carmen's attitude. "I don't want to know him. He's probably a bigger jerk than my stepdad."

But one time at her house, she and I were trying on makeup in front of the mirror when her thoughts became faraway.

"Do you think his cheeks were high like mine? Sometimes I wonder what he's like. Mamá says he was really handsome."

Obviously she was thinking about her dad.

Then there was Nora. Her dad was a college math professor, and to hear Nora tell it he was a genius. She totally idolized the guy—counting the days between visits with him. Maybe part of why she studied so hard was to get his attention.

Unfortunately her dad's new wife hated Nora and told her really mean things like: "Your dad doesn't have time to pick you up, take you home, and chauffeur you around. He has a new family to take care of."

Often after visiting her dad, Nora came over to my house and broke down in tears. She was afraid if her mom saw her she wouldn't let her go over her dad's anymore.

Finally there was María. Her dad was a totally loud

obnoxious guy who went by Tito. That was like a little kid's nickname, which was what her dad acted like. He was always leaving María's mom then pleading to come back, bringing pandas for María (she loves pandas), then losing his job, then leaving home again. . . . He was a mess. I couldn't imagine living with someone like that.

Like I said, our dads gave us endless conversation.

Because my stomach ached so much from the chocolate kisses, I skipped dinner that night. Instead I phoned the Sexies and told them about the Barbie and how I threw it against the wall. They all sympathized. By the time I went to bed, my stomach felt better.

# Chapter 10

## Frederick

Ever since the night Xio held my hand at the movies, I kept thinking: *Does that mean she likes me as girlfriend and boyfriend? I guess so. But do I like her that way?* I wasn't sure.

I liked talking with her. And I liked spending time with her. But how was it supposed to feel if you romantic-liked someone? It would help if they had classes to explain this stuff.

At my school in Wisconsin they had taught us all the technical info about sperm and eggs. It was kind of interesting, but now it seemed they skipped over some of the major things, like: *How do you know if you romantic-like someone in the first place?*

On the Monday after the movies, Victor walked up to me in the hall, wearing a big goofy grin. He winked at me, socking me on the shoulder. "You go, man!"

"Huh? What are you talking about?"

"You and Xio. Holding hands." He kept grinning at me. It was sort of annoying, but then he swung his arm around my shoulder—not in a headlock this time, instead like he admired me.

We walked down the hall like that. People stared at us, but I didn't mind a bit. In that moment I felt as if every single part of me, from my teeth to my toenails, was like, happy. I'd never felt that way with anyone—not with any of my friends back home . . . nor holding hands with Xio.

In early November, one day at lunch everyone at our table was excited about Thanksgiving plans—Nora about going to her dad's, José about visiting relatives in Tijuana, María about her dad being home for the holiday, and Carmen about spending it at Xio's.

"What are your plans?" Xio asked me.

"I guess we're going back to Wisconsin to my grandma's. That's where we always spend Thanksgiving."

I told the girls about the amazing cranberry-orange relish recipe Grandma and I had invented. It won first place at the county fair. And how she always saved the wishbone for she and I to break.

"Well, if you don't go," Xio said, "why don't you come to my house? Your parents, too. We always have lots of people over. It would be great."

"Thanks, but I'm sure we're going to my grandma's. We always do."

That afternoon when Mom came home from work (she'd finally gotten a job at an accounting firm) I ran downstairs, shouting, "Mom! We're going to Grandma's for Thanksgiving, aren't we?"

"No, honey," Mom called from the kitchen. "Not till Christmas."

"We're not?" I stared openmouthed as Mom unpacked groceries. "But we always do."

"I know. But we'll go to Grandma's at Christmas."

I dropped into a chair and crossed my arms. "But we *always* spend Thanksgiving at Grandma's."

"Honey, I know." Mom accidentally dropped a can of beans onto the counter. "But with the down payment on this house we can't afford two trips. We'll go at Christmas."

I sat moping. Sometimes I hated having moved away.

"Well, then . . . Xio invited us to her house. Is that okay?"

"No," Mom said sternly. "Mr. Garcia already invited us to his house."

"Mr. Garcia?" I asked, surprised. "The real estate agent?"

I couldn't believe Mom would pass up Grandma's *and* Xio's to spend the holiday with people we hardly knew. "Can't you tell him we're doing something else?"

"No." Mom crumpled up the plastic grocery bag. "I already accepted. That wouldn't be right."

"Well . . ." I thought fast. "Can I go to Xio's while you go to the Garcias'?"

"No, honey. He asked about you. He reminded me he has a son in your school." Her brow creased as if trying to recall his name. "Ignacio, I think."

I'd forgotten Mr. Garcia had once mentioned that. But now the name didn't ring a bell. He was probably some little sixth grader.

After dinner Xio phoned, hyper with excitement. "Did you find out if you're staying for Thanksgiving? Mami insists you come to our house—and your parents, too. Can you?"

"No . . ." I told Xio that Mom had already made other plans.

"That sucks," she groaned. I agreed.

Thanksgiving Thursday, the sky was overcast and gloomy. I didn't want to go to the Garcias' but what could I do? Mom wrapped up her special pumpkin cheesecake and we headed over.

The Garcias' rambling Spanish-style house was in a neighborhood on the other side of school. Mr. Garcia was big, like an ex-football player. I hated shaking hands with him because his grip squished my fingers. His wife was shorter than him but her hairdo made up for it—a big black tower.

Their older son, Juan, looked high school age. He slouched on the sofa watching a football game and grunted hi to us.

"Our younger son is probably on the phone," Mrs. Garcia explained. "Juan, can you get your brother?"

Without turning from the TV, Juan shouted toward the hall, "Hey, faggot!"

"Juan!" His dad reached out to cuff him but Juan ducked.

My shoulders tensed up. I was glad this wasn't *my* family.

Footsteps shuffled behind me and I turned. In front of me stood Iggy. I felt the color drain from my face.

"Ignacio," Mr. Garcia said, "this is Frederick."

"Yeah, I know." Iggy nodded to me, smiling with those undeniable dimples. "Hi."

I hesitated, silent. What would Xio and her friends say if they found out I'd spent Thanksgiving with Iggy? My throat tightened so much I could barely speak. "Um, hi."

"Juan, shut off the TV," Mrs. Garcia said. "Everyone come to the table."

"Why don't you and Iggy sit together?" Mr. Garcia told me. "So you can talk."

Oh, great. I kept my gaze down as I sat next to Iggy.

At the head of the table Mr. Garcia lifted his hand. "Let's all join hands for the blessing."

That meant I had to hold Iggy's. Crud. Normally holding another guy's hand to pray wouldn't have been a big deal. I'd done it loads of times in Sunday school. But this was different. What if Iggy really was gay?

He held his palm out to me, waiting. I noticed Juan staring at us and smirking. Mr. Garcia glowered at him.

I took Iggy's hand and silently uttered my own prayer. *Please, God, don't let anyone at school find out.*

Mr. Garcia's prayer went on forever. But I wasn't really listening. I was too busy peeking over at Iggy—for the first time getting a long look at him. His head was bowed. Brown bangs hung over his forehead, while his lips moved gently to his silent prayers. He had long eyelashes, and beneath his right eye hung a dark little freckle on his tan skin, like a teardrop.

He must've sensed me looking at him because his eyes blinked open and looked toward me.

Immediately I slammed my own eyes shut, my face growing hot as an oven. I hoped he hadn't caught me.

Thank God Mr. Garcia finally said, "Amen."

I quickly let go of Iggy's hand.

During the meal he and I didn't say much, other than *please* and *thanks* as we passed each other food.

When everyone had finished eating Mr. Garcia said, "Ignacio, why don't you take Frederick to your room and show him your parakeet."

His parakeet? I followed Iggy down the clay tile hallway, both of us silent. Did that mean he was nervous too? Maybe he thought I was weird for staring at him during prayers.

The walls of his room were covered with posters of boy bands—some of the same ones I liked. But I would never put posters of them up on my walls. Guys weren't supposed to do that. No wonder people thought Iggy was gay.

From a cage by the window came excited chirping.

"His name's Pete," Iggy said, leading me over.

The green-and-yellow parakeet fluttered on his swing. "He gets excited meeting people." Iggy turned to the bird. "Don't you, boy?"

Pete answered with a whistle. Iggy opened the cage and put his hand in, holding his index finger as a perch. Pete hopped onto it and Iggy slowly brought him out.

"Hi, fella," he told the bird in a calm, soft voice. "I brought someone to see you." He gently stroked the feathers as the bird stared at me and chirped, almost as if he understood Iggy.

"This is Frederick. Can you say Frederick?" Iggy brought the bird close to his lips and repeated my name several times till Pete squawked, "Ruck-rick."

It wasn't exactly Frederick, but it was close enough.

"How do you keep him from flying around?" I asked.

"I don't. Sometimes he does. Want to fly, pal?" Iggy extended his arm and Pete took off, flying around the room.

"What if he poops on something?" I giggled.

Iggy shrugged. "It's a great excuse for not having my homework."

That made me laugh. "How do you get him to fly back to you?"

"Just hold your finger out and he'll land on it. Go ahead. Try it."

A little nervously, I held my finger out. Pete circled a couple of times, eyeing me, and then landed. His tiny claws dug into my finger—not hurting, just tickling.

"Talk to him real soft," Iggy told me, "so he won't get nervous."

Slowly I brought Pete up close to my face, like

Iggy had. "Hey, fella. How's it going? You're not going to poop on my finger, are you?"

Gently I stroked his soft smooth feathers. "He's awesome, the way he looks at you like he knows what you're saying."

"Yeah," Iggy agreed. "He loves music, too. Why don't you pick something out?" He gestured to his CDs stacked against the wall and extended his finger for Pete to hop onto.

Iggy had a lot of discs, organized alphabetically by performer—a lot of the same artists I like, except I organize mine by type of music, for whatever mood I'm in.

"I love this!" I opened the case of one of my favorite female pop singers. "I've been wanting to get it."

We listened to the CD and played with Pete, getting him to fly across the room and come back to us. It was amazing.

"Do you have any pets?" Iggy asked.

"No," I told him. "My mom's afraid they'll stir up my asthma."

It surprised me I admitted that to Iggy. I guess I was starting to feel more comfortable with him. Even the whole *Is he gay?* thing had stopped fluttering around my head.

Iggy asked me my hobbies, and when I told him I

liked to sketch houses he asked me to draw him one. He had a sketch pad since he likes to draw too— mostly people—and he sketched me. It came out really good.

I totally lost track of time until Mrs. Garcia tapped on the door, my mom at her side.

"You draw very well," Mom told Iggy when I showed her the drawing he'd done. "Unfortunately we have to head home, honey." She stroked the back of my neck. "The Garcias are going to church."

I didn't really want to leave. As Mom and Mrs. Garcia headed back toward the living room, I reluctantly said bye to Pete and asked Iggy, "Can I keep the drawing of me?"

"Sure." He grinned, dimples crinkling his cheeks.

"You can keep my house drawing," I told him. "Or throw it out if you don't want it."

"I'll keep it," he told me.

As I looked back at him I started feeling mixed up inside. I'd had a really fun time with him, but what would happen when I saw him in school?

"Don't worry." His dimples faded as if he'd read my mind. "You don't have to talk to me at school if you don't want. I know the stuff other kids say about me."

I glanced down at the carpet, embarrassed. But why? *I* hadn't said anything bad about him. Yeah, but I hadn't stuck up for him either. And yet how could I stand up for him if I didn't know whether or not he really was gay? I wanted to ask him "Is it true?" But what if he answered yes?

I gulped to swallow the knot in my throat. "Of course I'll talk to you," I told him, though I wasn't sure I really meant it.

"Okay." He grinned, the dimples growing in his cheeks again.

On the drive home Dad asked from the front seat, "So, what did you boys do all afternoon?"

"You should've come see! He's got a parakeet he lets outside his cage. It's really cool. We listened to music. He did a drawing of me." I reached over to show him.

"Iggy seems like a very nice boy." Mom smiled.

Dad glanced up from the drawing into the rearview. "Do you know him very well?"

The way he asked the question gave me an odd feeling. Did he suspect Iggy was gay? Maybe I was just being paranoid.

"Not really," I said and tugged at my seat belt.

When I got home I pinned Iggy's drawing on my bulletin board. For the rest of the evening I lay on my bedroom carpet, playing discs of the artist we'd listened to, singing along with the lyrics, and wishing I'd asked Iggy "Are you gay?"

And if he was, how did he know?

# Chapter 11

## Xio

Like every year, Thanksgiving was a huge event at my house, with tons of food and people.

The day began as I took Stevie with me to our neighbor's, Mrs. Buenaventura's, to buy tortillas. She makes them fresh by hand for the holidays, so they're a gazillion times better than store-bought. Steaming hot, with a little bit of butter and sprinkled salt, they nearly melt in your mouth. Her entire house smelled of warm *masa*—so delicious I didn't want to leave.

But I needed to return home to help Mami prepare her best-turkey-on-earth recipe, *mole poblano de guajolote*. The sauce mixes six flavors of chili peppers, roasted onions, sautéed garlic, juicy ripe tomatoes, cloves, cinnamon, and at the very end, the magical ingredient . . . melted chocolate. My mouth was watering the entire time.

The first guests arrived at noon. Of course, Mami

had invited Rodolfo. He brought her a beautiful fall bouquet—brilliant orange roses, yellow sunflowers, and red daisies. Propped on his arm was his mom—a silver-haired lady, stooped over a cane, with glasses that gave her goldfish eyes.

Next arrived Mami's best friend, Beatriz, who brought caramelized yams and her five-year-old son, Cesar.

They were followed by Mr. Flores, our bachelor neighbor across the street who's always taking in stray cats. He brought Corona beer and pumpkin pie.

I'd invited Carmen, like I do every year. She hates to spend holidays at home because her two older brothers get drunk and start fighting. She brought some *pico de gallo* sauce and her overnight stuff so she could spend the night.

When she met Rodolfo, she turned totally goo-goo-eyed crazy. Usually she acted so cool about guys, but now I had to pry her away, dragging her into the kitchen.

"*Qué paso?*" Mami asked as we staggered in, giggling.

"She's fallen in lust with Rodolfo," I explained.

"Mrs. Juárez," Carmen told Mami. "He's so hot!"

"*Gracias,* Carmen." Mami gave her head a little shake. "Can you girls set the table, please?"

I suggested we sit outside since it was warm and sunny. Rodolfo and Mr. Flores carried the dining table and chairs onto the back patio, while Beatriz, Carmen, and I spread out the tablecloths and place settings. Carmen kept bumping into me, unable to take her eyes off Rodolfo.

When we finally sat down, we bowed our heads while Mami gave the blessing. Then she asked if anyone wanted to add any words of their own.

"*Gracias* also for new friends," Rodolfo said.

I peeked up and saw him squeeze Mami's hand. Silently I gave thanks for Frederick, wishing he could've been with us.

After Beatriz gave thanks for good health and Mr. Flores for good neighbors, Cesar asked, "Can we start eating now?"

Everyone laughed and we began our feast. It was all so delicious—especially the chocolate sauce. Not till I thought my stomach would pop did I stop eating.

After our meal I took Rodolfo's mom to Mami's room so she could lie down for a nap. Rodolfo helped clear the table until Mami told him to go relax with Mr. Flores. Carmen and I helped Beatriz and Mami clean up the kitchen and load the dishwasher.

Then Carmen and I went to my room and collapsed

into bed, patting our stomachs, complaining about how much we'd eaten, and listening to CDs till we fell asleep. After we woke up we watched music videos, getting up to sing and dance, till we got hungry for more pumpkin pie.

Beatriz, Cesar, and Mr. Flores had left. Rodolfo's mom was watching TV with Stevie in the living room.

As I approached the kitchen door, I heard Mami laughing softly inside. I put a finger to my lips, signaling Carmen to keep quiet. Then I cracked the swing door open a smidge. Carmen's cheek pressed against mine. We peered in and saw Mami putting plates away. As Rodolfo handed them to her he kissed her neck, while Mami giggled.

"What I wouldn't give to be her," Carmen whispered over my shoulder.

After getting some pie from the kitchen, we went back to my room and Carmen phoned Victor. Meanwhile I started cleaning out my closet—my big project for the weekend, at Mami's insistence. When Carmen got off the phone, I called Frederick and told him all about our Thanksgiving.

"And what about yours?" I asked.

"It was okay," he said. "Nothing special." Sometimes he can be *so* not talkative. I don't know how anyone can be like that.

Carmen stayed over the entire weekend. We carted my old clothes to Goodwill, decorated our feet with henna tattoos, took Stevie to swing at the playground, and went to the mall. I love Carmen. I have so much fun with her.

At lunch on Monday everyone talked about their weekend.

"I learned how to change a flat tire," José beamed, "on our drive home from Tijuana."

"How butch!" Carmen squeezed José's bicep.

"Would you grow up?" José pulled her arm away.

From that point the conversation turned downhill.

"Tito still hasn't come home," María said, staring down at her uneaten lunch. She'd phoned me over the weekend to say Tito and her mom had once again had a fight.

"The only time I got to spend with my dad," Nora mumbled, "was him driving me home."

Her stepmom hadn't let her stay after Thanksgiving dinner, claiming there wasn't any room for Nora to sleep because of her own visiting relatives. Nora had come over to my house crying on Friday and told Carmen and me all about it.

Now everyone turned quiet at our lunch table till José asked Frederick, "How about you? What did you do?"

"Nothing much," he said softly. "Just went to someone's house. That's all."

I stared at him, wondering again: *Why is he being so vague?* After hearing Nora and Maria's heart-wrenching stories, I was worried. Had something bad happened to him?

The others looked toward me and I looked back at them, till Carmen spoke up. "Well, Frederick, whose house did you go to?"

"No one . . ." He shifted in his seat. "Just our real estate agent, Mr. Garcia."

Nora adjusted her glasses. "You mean Iggy's dad?"

I leaned toward Frederick, a little shocked. "You went to *Iggy's?*"

"Um, yeah . . ." Frederick said, turning redder than cranberry sauce. "I mean, I didn't know it was his dad."

The rest of us glanced at each other again. Why hadn't he said anything earlier?

Then out of the blue Carmen asked, "Are you gay?"

"Carmen!" I yelled, but she kept her eyes narrowed on Frederick.

He hesitated an instant, his eyes darting between Carmen and us. Then he sat up and shouted at her, "No!"

I'd never really seen him mad before, but I

couldn't blame him. Everyone knows calling somebody gay is just about the worst thing you can say to them. And *asking* someone if they're gay is like telling them you think they *are* gay.

"Carmen," I repeated, "shut up!"

Then the bell rang. Frederick leaped up, pushed away his chair, and stormed off.

"You are so stupid," I told Carmen. "Why did you say that?"

"Well . . ." She turned to me, trying to act innocent. "Why didn't he tell us he went to Iggy's?"

"Because it's none of your business."

She backed her chair away. "I simply asked him a question."

"Fine!" I told her. "I'll ask Victor if he's gay."

"Go ahead." Carmen grabbed her tray. "What do I care? I know he's not."

At that moment, I hated Carmen. She could *so* get on my nerves sometimes. For the rest of the day I refused to talk to her.

After school I looked for Frederick, but he didn't show up at his locker or at soccer. As soon as I got home I phoned and told him, "I think Carmen is so stupid for what she said. I'm not talking to her again till she apologizes to you."

"It's no big deal," he said. But his voice sounded hurt.

Cancerians are sensitive—more than other signs. Being sensitive is one of the things I like about Frederick.

And it doesn't mean he's gay.

# Chapter 12

## Frederick

Why'd I get so mad just because Carmen asked if I was gay? I mean, I know people say stupid stuff like that all the time. But how was I supposed to react? Why'd she ask me that anyway?

After school I only wanted to go home. In my room I went online, hoping to talk to Marcie or Janice or William. They never asked me dumb questions like that. But none of them were logged on. I slumped down in my chair, wishing I'd never left Wisconsin—and wishing I'd never gone to Iggy's.

I glanced up from the computer to his drawing of me, tacked on my bulletin board. Was he really gay? And I couldn't help keep wondering, if he was, how did he know?

With my hand trembling a little, I clicked my browser on, moved my fingers to the keyboard, and typed three letters: G . . . A . . . Y.

Within seconds, a page came up listing 57,386,552 entries. I gulped. Where would I start?

The entries were mostly news stories about gay marriage, court cases, adult stuff. Suddenly an entry jumped out at me. A teenage basketball player had just come out at his high school.

I clicked the link to the story and read it over and over, each time coming back to one part where the reporter asked the boy: How had he known he was gay?

"I always felt different from other kids," the boy answered. "And besides, I thought guys were cuter."

Below the quote was a photo of a teenager in his team tank top, smiling happily. He didn't look gay. I mean, he just looked normal. And he was cute.

My hands started sweating as I scrolled up and down the story. Finally I clicked the links at the end, leading to all sorts of teen-oriented stuff—youth groups, parents' organizations, even churches that accepted gay people.

Suddenly I heard the door downstairs. "Honey? You home?"

Mom! I jumped from my chair and yelled, "I'm doing some homework!" as I ran to my door and quietly closed it. Then I scrambled back to my browser and carefully cleared my tracks.

"You look like something's troubling you," Mom

told me at dinner. "Anything wrong?"

"No, nothing's wrong," I answered. But inside I wondered, *What* is *wrong with me?* Why had I read that story about the teenage basketball player so many times I could see his face without even closing my eyes?

After dinner I was doing homework in my room when Dad came in. "Hey, sport."

He calls me "sport" sometimes. I'm not crazy about it, but it could be worse—something *really* goofy, like "my little grasshopper."

"Anything you want to talk about?" he asked, sitting down on the bed.

"Um, no." I glanced down at the carpet but I could still feel his gaze on me.

"Is everything okay at school?"

"Yeah." I nodded.

"How are things going between you and Xio?"

Apparently he and Mom had decided Xio was my girlfriend. I flashed him a glance, hoping he wouldn't go into one of those doofy birds-and-bees talks like dads in movies do.

"Everything's fine, Dad."

He scratched his chest. "How's soccer going? I think you're getting taller."

"Really?" I said, sitting up.

He nodded. "It looks to me like you are. We

should keep track like we used to."

In our old house Dad had measured me with pencil marks on my closet door frame. When I was little it was exciting, but during the last couple of years my lack of progress got pretty depressing. I'd almost begun wondering if I'd actually been adopted from pygmies.

"Let's start keeping track again." Dad reached into the pencil holder on my desk. "What's today's date?" He waved me over to stand against the closet door frame. "The third?"

The pencil brushed across the top of my head. I turned as he marked the date with his left hand. (Dad's a lefty.)

"You want to do some golfing this Saturday?" he asked. "Just the two of us?"

"Sure," I told him. It had been several weeks since I'd gone. I just hoped he wouldn't ask any more questions about Xio and me.

At lunch next day Xio and Carmen weren't talking. They wouldn't even look at each other. Xio sat on one side of the table; Carmen on the other. Nora, José, María, and I sat between them, turning back and forth as Xio and Carmen vied for our attention. Example:

Xio: "You guys want to go to a movie Saturday?"

(She purposely avoids looking at Carmen.) "Of course *certain people* known for saying stupid things aren't invited."

Carmen (steam practically flaring out her nostrils): "Sorry I can't make it. I'm having a sleepover Saturday. Everyone's invited *except* those who keep making a huge deal over something that isn't."

Me: *This is nuts.*

I mean, I was still mad at Carmen too, but I wasn't making everyone else suffer for it.

I almost decided to sit with Victor and his friends, but I didn't want to bail on Xio, especially since she'd stood up for me. Instead I watched the excruciatingly slow lunchroom clock tick the minutes till the bell.

After school I hurried to the soccer field, eager to play and take my mind off everything. But instead it seemed like the guys kept cursing *"Maricón!"* every time someone stole a ball or "That was gay!" whenever someone missed a goal.

Were they saying more of that stuff? Or was it just bothering me more?

I was happy when Saturday—and golf with Dad—arrived. We always played only for fun, never keeping score, since his game's ten times better than mine. I used rental clubs but Dad had his own personal left-handed set. Golf was our time to talk about stuff—sports, weather, school, things at his job, news events, almost anything.

Today I watched him swing and asked, "What makes some people left-handed?"

I didn't realize that question would lead me to the other question I *really* wanted to ask.

"Some unidentified gene," Dad said as we watched his ball fly across the fairway.

He had explained genes to me before—how microscopic code in our cells determines our eye and hair color, how tall we are, lots of stuff about us.

"But *why*?" I insisted. "Why are some people left-handed when almost everyone else is right-handed?"

Dad shrugged. "That's how nature works. Everyone's different—and in that way we're all alike. It keeps a species strong, though people don't always realize that. When I was little, I always got picked on for being a lefty. One teacher even tried to make me use my other hand. It made me think something was wrong with me."

"For real?" I squinted in the sun as we started walking.

"In the really old days," Dad continued, "people used to think lefties were evil. You know that's where the word *sinister* comes from? Lefties, albinos, the mentally retarded—anyone who's somehow different has at one time or another been considered bad or evil."

It suddenly struck me this was the chance to slip in my question. Despite the lump in my throat I tried to sound casual. "Um . . . what about gay people? Do you think they're bad?"

Dad gazed over his shoulder at me with that same odd look he'd given me in the rearview mirror on the ride home from Iggy's. Meanwhile I kept my face blank, trying to appear as though it was the most normal question on earth.

"I guess gay people aren't any different than the rest of us," Dad said at last. "Except they're gay."

Although his words were reassuring, his look made me wish I hadn't asked. After that I decided to drop it. The sun was starting to get to me anyway.

Monday morning in first period, Carmen and Xio still weren't talking. Would I be able to endure another tense, miserable week of this?

At lunch Carmen plopped onto the seat across from Xio and said: "Look, I'm sorry, okay?"

Nora, José, María, and I turned to look at Xio. She pursed her lips, looking thoughtfully up toward the ceiling. Then she said: "It's not me you need to apologize to."

Carmen glared at her, sighed, and turned to me.

"Frederick, I'm sorry I asked if you're gay. Okay?"

"Okay," I said, the tension easing from my shoulders.

Then Xio reached under the table and I felt her lay her hand on mine, giving it a squeeze. She must've been as thankful the feud had ended as I was.

Except I had a new worry: Was she going to start holding my hand at school now?

# Chapter 13

## Xio

I hadn't planned to take hold of Frederick's hand, but I was so ecstatic that Carmen had *finally* apologized to him. I'd known she hadn't really meant to shoot off her mouth with him. But she's a Scorpio, and Scorpios can be *very* possessive. Obviously she's jealous that Frederick and I are becoming so close.

Anyway, I'm glad I held Frederick's hand again, because sometimes I worry, *Does he really like me as much as I like him?*

One night online I asked the Sexies what they thought. I immediately got bombarded by IMs.

PandaFan_SC (María): `Doesn't he phone you all the time?`

Soccerina_CA (José): **Didn't he bring you a bite-size Snickers the other day?**

QuizWhiz23 (Nora): `Didn't he help you with your civil rights report?`

94

LeoGirlsRule (Me): **Yeah, yeah, yeah. I guess you're right.**

But then why doesn't he make a move? At this rate I'll be as stooped and shriveled as Rodolfo's mom before Frederick and I even kiss.

At the supermarket one evening with Mami, I spotted an astrology love-signs book and looked up the Leo-Cancer match.

> *A Leo woman pounces with all fours and gives her heart passionately.*

"Yep," I mumbled to myself. "Got that right."

> *In contrast, the Cancer man tends to be a romantic daydreamer. To the Leo huntress, he may seem as elusive as the clouds.*

Boy, that nailed it.

> *So how can you succeed at conquering your Cancer man?*

I flipped the page, nearly tearing it.

> *First and foremost, let your insecure Cancerian know how much you admire him.*
> *Do you like what he's wearing? His smile? Tell him so. Nothing will draw him to you more certainly than sincere approval.*
> *Compliment his ability to listen. (No one is a better listener than a Cancer.) Ask his advice.*

*Is there something you want him to do? Make him think it's his idea.*

*Allow your Cancer guy to show his best side: empathy, understanding, and an exceptional ability to give suggestions.*

*And remember, Cancerians don't rush headlong into anything. The Cancer man is essentially skittish, but once he gives himself over, you'll have a constant and devoted companion.*

Companion? I wanted a *boyfriend,* not a dog. I wanted passion! *Amor!*

"Xio?" Mami called, already at the cash register.

I closed the book and returned it to the rack. But as we drove home I got an idea.

"Mami?" I asked. "Can I have a party before we go to Abuelita's for the holidays? I haven't had one since my birthday."

Mami had been humming but now paused while considering my question. She hums when she's in a good mood, and she'd been humming a lot since taking my advice to date Rodolfo. So I was pretty sure she'd say yes about the party—and she did.

Once home I quickly helped put away the groceries and ran to phone the Sexies, starting with Carmen.

As we talked about the party, she came up with a

wicked new romantic way to play Musical Chairs. Carmen can be *so* bad—in a good way.

We decided each Sexy would invite one boy. Obviously Carmen would invite Victor and I'd invite Frederick. Now we had to convince the other girls. Carmen stayed on the phone as I conferenced in one after the other.

At first Nora whined, "I've got too much homework to do."

But then I suggested she invite Kiki. He's one of the soccer boys but also a bit of a brainiac, like her.

"Do you think he'd come?" Nora's voice perked up.

"I'll get Victor to make him come," Carmen said, and Nora was in.

Next I dialed José. While waiting for her to answer, Carmen and I debated what boy she might like.

"Have you noticed?" I asked. "She keeps bumping into Pepe when she plays soccer? I don't think it's by accident."

But when I told that to José, she complained, "He's the one who bumps into *me*!" Then she softened. "Maybe you're right. Okay, I'll invite him."

Carmen and I had one last call to make. We'd figured it would be the hardest.

Sure enough, María gasped, "*Ay, Dios!* Invite a boy to a party? I've never done that. Who would I ask?"

"What about Gordo from soccer?" I suggested.

He was a polite, heavyset guy who always carried licorice in his pocket and who was about as timid as María.

"But he's so big!" María exclaimed.

"Yeah, but sweet," I pointed out.

"That's probably because of all the licorice he eats." María giggled but then turned serious. "I don't know. What if he tries something funny?"

"Stop worrying," Carmen told her. "If he does, just feed him."

"Okay." María gave a sigh. "But will you come with me to ask him?"

Knowing it was a big step for her, I agreed.

Our mission had been accomplished. Everyone was on board—at least on the girls' side.

Before hanging up, Carmen offered to bring her Polaroid for party pics. Then I began planning how to invite Frederick, recalling what I'd read in the love-signs book.

When I walked into first period next day, Frederick was organizing his notebook.

"Your hair looks nice," I whispered.

"Huh?" He blushed, turning pink like he does. "Thanks."

At lunch I told him, "I like your shirt. Is that teal? It goes really good with your eyes. I wish I had blue eyes like yours."

"Um, thanks," he replied again.

After soccer that afternoon I said, "Can I ask your advice about a problem?"

"Um, sure."

He listened eagerly as I began. "My problem is that my favorite time of year is the holidays, with all the parties. Except no one is having a party this year. I don't know what to do."

"Well . . ." He raised his eyebrows in a puzzled look. "Can't you have one?"

"Oh, my God, that's such a great idea! Frederick, you're a genius."

"Um . . . not really."

"Yes, you are. Stop being so modest. Will you come?"

"I would, except we're going to Wisconsin for Christmas."

"Don't worry. We'll have the party before you go. It'll be so much fun!"

On my way home I hummed like Mami, my mind wandering to boys I'd kissed in the past—nonrelatives, I mean, since in my family everyone always pecked everybody on the cheek. That didn't count.

My first kiss had been with Gustavito Mendoza in fifth grade—centuries ago. He was this really shy boy (even shyer than Frederick) who rode my school bus. One day Carmen dared me to sit in back with the boys, so I did—next to Gustavito. All the girls were giggling and the boys gave him a hard time.

At the end of the ride I leaned over to him. His skin smelled like sweetened condensed milk. I kissed him on the cheek and he broke into a big smile.

After that I was dying to know what it would taste like to kiss on the mouth. But that didn't happen till sixth grade, with Javier Sandoval—my first official boyfriend. One day after class, Carmen kept a lookout while Javier and I went behind the big oak in back of school. I remember being disappointed the kiss didn't taste like much, but it was really just a peck on the lips. No tongue.

My first French kiss didn't come till seventh grade, with Gloria's brother Marco, before they moved away to Nevada. He and I weren't really boyfriend and girlfriend, but I used to see him all the time at Gloria's. He was a year older and really cute (though nowhere near as cute as Frederick).

One day he was pouring me a Coke while Gloria was in the bathroom. Suddenly he turned to me and said, "Want to make out?"

"Okay." I shrugged, my heart thumping.

He put down his glass and then he was tapping his tongue against mine, cold and sweet like Coke. But after that Gloria's family moved to Nevada.

Now I wondered, *What will Frederick kiss like?*

I bet he'd be gentle as a pony and his breath sweet as honey.

"I don't have anything to wear for the party," I told Mami at dinner.

"What about your black dress?"

"Everyone's seen that." I scooped an enchilada from the serving dish and picked at the melted cheese, thinking.

"Can I borrow one of your dresses?" I asked. I wasn't quite as tall as Mami, but otherwise we were the same size—and I knew exactly what I'd wear.

Mami glanced up from the *frijoles* she was serving Stevie.

"Please, please, please?" I pressed my hands together, begging till she gave in.

As soon as I finished dinner I bolted to her closet and pulled out my favorite shimmering dress.

# Chapter 14

## Frederick

In Wisconsin my friends and I didn't have many parties, other than birthdays. The most fun was Janice's last one, when we had a dance contest. Since Janice and I memorized steps from music videos all the time, she and I won easily.

"Will there be dancing at your party?" I asked Xio.

"Of course! What's a party without dancing?"

Mom suggested I take her a holiday gift. "Any idea what she'd like?"

"Chocolate," I replied. That was a no-brainer.

The night of the party Dad drove me over to Xio's. When she answered the door, the sight of her made me catch my breath.

She looked about sixteen the way she'd done her makeup, with bright lipstick and eye shadow, her hair tumbling over the straps of her shiny red dress. I'd never before seen her bare shoulders.

"Hi." She twirled on the heels of her wrap-up

sandals, making her dress flare. "What do you think?"

"Huh?" I stood staring. "Um, you look great."

Her smile grew wide as a toothpaste model's. "Thanks. You look great too. Come on in." She took hold of my hand. She seemed to be doing that a lot lately.

Victor and some of the guys from soccer—Pepe, Kiki, and Gordo—hovered in the dining room, sipping sodas and chowing down snacks. Meanwhile, across the foyer in the living room the girls chatted. It was the first time I'd seen them all in party dresses. José hardly ever even wore skirts to school, much less a dress.

"Hi, Frederick!" Nora, María, José, and Carmen waved.

I took off my jacket and gave Xio the box of chocolates I'd brought.

"Oh, you're so sweet!" she gushed.

I quickly shoved my hands in my pockets.

"Hey, Rico!" Victor shouted, waving me into the dining room. "How you doing?"

I walked over, we clasped palms in the air, and he swung his arm around my shoulder. Leaning into him, I once again felt his muscled side pressed against my skinny chest. His breath felt warm on my cheek, smelling sweetly of tortilla chips.

"Don't move!" Xio yelled. "I want to take a picture of you two." She lifted a Polaroid camera. *"Queso!"* she said (I guessed that meant "cheese") and the flash went off.

"It came out good," Victor said as we crowded around Xio, watching the picture expose.

I thought it turned out better than good. The photo of Victor and me was awesome. I really wanted it but I told Victor he could have it.

"Thanks," he said, but then reconsidered. "No, you take it."

"Tear it in half," Pepe said sarcastically. He was always cracking jokes at soccer — a real wise guy.

"Take a couple of Frederick and me," Xio said. She handed the camera to Kiki — one of the quieter guys at soccer.

"Put your arm around me," Xio whispered as she stood next to me.

At first I laid my hand on her shoulder, but it felt sort of embarrassing to touch her bare skin there, so instead I shifted my arm to her waist.

Our photo came out great, except Victor had provided Xio a set of horns behind her head.

"Victor!" she shouted, swatting him. "Kiki, take another one. Victor, get away!"

The next photo lacked his fingers. She gave it to me and took another one for herself.

"Hey, guys?" Carmen called from the living room. "Come sit with us."

"We're eating," Gordo told her, chomping on a potato chip. His real name was Samuel. For several weeks I'd thought Gordo was his real name, till Xio told me *gordo* means "fat guy."

"Doesn't he mind that people call him that?" I'd asked her.

"No." She laughed. "We give everyone a nickname—not in a mean way. It's part of our culture."

Now José yelled from the living room, "You guys have been eating since you got here."

"So?" Pepe laughed. "Isn't that why you invited us?"

Carmen said something in Spanish to the girls. A moment later, the troop marched into the dining room, swooping up the bowls of salsa and chips, while Xio grabbed the sodas.

"No!" the boys protested, but the girls ignored them. And the boys followed into the living room, mumbling and grumbling.

Everyone crowded around the coffee table. We joked, ate, took goofy photos, and listened to both American and Spanish CDs.

Every once in a while Xio's mom came out with Xio's little brother and asked, "Is everyone having a good time?"

"Yes, Mami." Xio waved her away. "Stop worrying."

And each time her little brother begged to stay with us, as Xio's mom pulled him back to the bedroom.

We continued joking and eating till Gordo emptied the last crumbs from each bowl into his hand and moaned, "All the chips are gone."

María stood to get some more, but Xio grabbed her arm. "Enough eating! It's time to dance."

Carmen and Victor argued about what CD to play. Finally they agreed on a Spanish album and Xio pulled couples onto their feet.

Then she extended her hand to me. "Frederick, come on!"

I'd been watching Victor and Carmen close dancing to the song, arm in arm. Back in Wisconsin we'd never danced that way.

"It's called merengue," Xio explained. "It means meringue, like the pie." She giggled, grabbing my hand. "You move your hips like you're beating egg whites."

She pulled me close to her—closer than I'd ever faced a girl, so close her hair tickled my neck and my ears grew warm from nervousness. Fortunately the song had a fast beat so we kept moving.

"That's good," Xio whispered in my ear. "It's all about the hips. Look at Victor."

I turned and watched. His shoulders remained level but his hips rolled in waves to the music's rhythm. I tried to imitate him though I doubted I could.

"You've got it." Xio's body pressed soft against me.

I'd become aware I was sweating, though I wasn't sure if it was from dancing or from watching Victor lead Carmen.

He was a great dancer. As his hips moved with hers, it almost looked like he and Carmen were doing more than dancing.

Not wanting to gawk I looked away, but noticed everyone else staring at them too. He and Carmen must have known it. How could they not have, as each couple stopped to watch openmouthed?

"*Madre Santisima,*" María murmured, covering her eyes but obviously peeking between her fingers.

When the song ended, Victor parted from Carmen and the rest of us exhaled one huge sigh— disappointed, and also relieved.

"*Ay, ay, ay,*" Nora exclaimed, fanning herself, while the other girls teased Carmen.

She picked up her drink and gulped it thirstily, then scooped an ice cube from the cup and rolled it across her throat.

Meanwhile the boys praised Victor as he ran a hand through his hair. Then he held out his palm and each of us slapped it.

"Let's play Musical Chairs," Xio exclaimed.

*"Orale!"* the boys cheered, collapsing into the sofa.

"Except," Xio added, "whoever's left standing has to pick somebody to take into the closet."

"No way," the boys groaned. "Forget it! That's dumb."

*What would happen inside the closet?* I wondered, though I had a pretty good suspicion.

Xio waved aside the boys' protests. "The couple has to stay in for fifteen seconds."

"Um, can I use the bathroom?" I interrupted, hoping maybe I could sit out the game without anyone noticing.

"We won't start till you get back," Xio told me. "Hurry up."

My heart pounded as I locked the bathroom door behind me. The fact was I'd never kissed any girl before. When other boys talked about stuff like that, it never really interested me. And it wasn't at the top of my goals for tonight either.

I began nervously rearranging the little clam-shaped soaps and folding the towels on the rod, wondering: *But why don't I want to kiss any of the girls?*

"Frederick," Xio shouted. "Hurry up! We're waiting."

"He's scared," I heard one of the boys say.

"He's gay," another boy chimed in.

Everyone laughed, then Carmen said, "Don't give me a dirty look. I didn't say it this time."

*Is that what's the matter with me?* I wondered. *But how could they know that?*

"Frederick!" Xio shouted again.

My forehead was beading up with sweat. I didn't want to go out but I didn't want them joking about me either.

"Come on," I told myself. "Fifteen seconds isn't that long." Mustering all my willpower, I opened the door.

"Everybody ready?" Xio said from beside the stereo. She started the CD.

Everyone began circling till the music stopped. Then everybody scrambled, laughing and screaming, throwing themselves onto the sofa or chairs.

Nora was the only one left standing. As she adjusted her glasses I turned my head away, praying she wouldn't pick me.

Fortunately she pointed to Kiki. The other girls clapped and started chanting, "Ki-ki! Ki-ki!"

The boys hooted and whistled, tugging at Kiki's arms and pushing him off the sofa.

Although I felt sorry for the guy, at least *I'd* escaped.

Driven by cheers and laughter, Kiki accompanied

Nora behind the white closet door. A moment later, the countdown began: "Fifteen, fourteen . . ."

As I counted, I realized fifteen seconds was way the heck longer than I'd ever thought.

"Zero!" everyone finally shouted. Nora and Kiki emerged, both fumbling to adjust their glasses, their tan skin blushing a shade darker, but . . . at least they were smiling.

*Maybe it's not so bad,* I thought. Then why was my stomach grinding?

Since Kiki was chosen the past round, this time it was his turn to start the CD. I circled the room with the others, watching him like a hawk. When the music stopped, I leaped for a seat.

Victor was the one left standing this time, though it seemed he may have done it on purpose. As he scanned the group, it reminded me of soccer and how excited I felt when he picked me for his team. Now, what if he chose me to go into the closet with him?

Wait a minute. Where on earth had that idea come from?

Victor glanced from girl to girl, tapping a finger to his chin as if trying to decide whom to pick, while Carmen perched a hand on her hip, indignant.

"You'd better pick me," she scolded. And of course he did. She leaped from the sofa, smiling proudly.

"Call us in the morning." Victor gave a sly grin and pulled the closet door behind them.

As everyone counted down, I imagined Victor's arms encircling Carmen as they kissed, and I recalled his sweet tortilla-chip breath.

"Zero!" the group shouted, jarring my thoughts.

I expected Victor to burst from the closet, smiling triumphantly. But the door stayed closed. The seconds passed. The rest of us glanced at one another, unsure what to do.

"Hey," Xio called nervously. "Come on out!"

From inside the closet we heard Carmen hiss, "Vic-tor!" An instant later, she stumbled out, pulling up her shoulder strap.

Victor trailed behind her, grinning ear to ear as the other boys laughed and slapped him five.

Carmen strutted over to the CD player and once again the music started. This time María lost. *"Ay, Dios mío."* She turned tomato red, wringing her hands together as her eyes darted from boy to boy, till finally Gordo volunteered. "I'll go."

Everyone applauded as he accompanied María to the closet and closed the door.

But almost instantly it swung open again. A barrage of Spanish fired back and forth as the closet door got pulled and pushed, closed, open, closed.

"We'd better start," Xio suggested. "Fifteen, fourteen . . ."

We only made it to four seconds before the door burst open again.

"We're done," María announced, scampering across the room. "That's enough."

Behind her, Gordo lumbered out, rolling his eyes.

Pepe lost the next round and glanced at Xio as if to pick her. But she shook her head no and gestured toward José.

Had the girls rigged this whole game? I realized that meant there was no way I was getting out of it. My heart sank to my stomach.

But why? All the other boys seemed able to get through it.

While the countdown proceeded, sweat trickled down my forehead. As Pepe and José emerged from the closet, everybody cheered. Everyone except me.

Once again the music started. When it stopped, Xio was left standing. What a huge surprise.

Her bright brown eyes smiled at me. "Frederick?"

As I tried to return her smile, everyone else whooped and whistled.

Victor pushed me out of my seat, proudly clapping me on the back. But why wasn't *I* feeling proud?

Slowly I inched toward the closet, while inside Xio pushed the coats aside, creating a cozy alcove.

"Close the door," she whispered. But my hand wouldn't move.

Xio gave a giggle and reached for the knob, sealing us in darkness. Her warmth radiated toward me, carrying the scent of her perfume.

Outside the muffled countdown had begun, but all I heard was the pounding of my heart. I waited, legs trembling, thinking: *Maybe if I don't do anything Xio won't either.*

But then her clean-smelling hair tickled my ear and I knew she was bending down to me. Instinctively I tilted my head up. Her skin brushed my cheek. And then her lips touched mine, pressing gently. Every nerve in my mouth tingled.

*If only Victor could see me now,* I thought, *he'd proudly pat my back and put his arm around me.* And suddenly it was no longer Xio, but Victor kissing me.

Startled, I jumped away backward. What had made me think that?

"Zero!" the crowd shouted outside.

I fumbled for my balance, stumbling out the door. Everyone cheered and Victor really did clap me on the back, obviously unaware of what I'd been imagining.

For the rest of the evening I pretended to have fun as we listened to CDs, ate more chips, and watched MTV. But inside my head I couldn't stop thinking about what I'd imagined inside the closet, till at last Xio's mom came out and said it was getting late.

At the door Xio told me, "Thanks." And a soft kiss landed on my cheek.

Kiki's parents gave me a ride to my house. Inside Mom and Dad were holding hands on the sofa, watching TV.

"How was the party?" Mom asked cheerfully.

"Okay." I started toward the stairs. "I'm going to bed. Good night."

"Frederick?" Mom called after me.

Reluctantly I turned around.

"Honey?" Her forehead crinkled with concern. "Is everything all right?"

"Um, yeah." I gave a shrug. "I'm just tired. We danced a lot."

But I really wasn't the least bit tired. As I undressed and brushed my teeth, I was wide awake, wondering: *Why had I thought of Victor while kissing Xio?*

Afraid of the answer, I climbed into bed and turned out the light, tossing and turning beneath my sheets and trying to get to sleep.

# Chapter 15

## Xio

He actually kissed me! And we're not even stooped and old yet. His lips were tender as marshmallows, his breath sweet as honey, and his kiss the most gentle in history.

After everyone had gone home, Mami helped me clean up the party mess of cups and stuff. And I danced around the kitchen, twirling in circles, shouting, *"Amar es vivir! Vivir es amar!"* (That's a Spanish saying: "To love is to live! To live is to love!")

The following week I could barely concentrate at school. First, because each time I thought of Frederick (which was nearly every second) my skin tingled as if brushed by a thousand butterfly wings. Second, because of my excitement about going to Mexico.

Saturday morning Mami, Stevie, and I checked our jumble of suitcases, bags, and presents at the airport and flew to Guadalajara, the pearl of western Mexico, to gather at my *abuelitos'*. My grandparents (on Mami's side) are the cornerstone of our family, and during the holidays we all gather there.

When we arrived I ran into Abuelita's arms, breathing in her one-and-only smell of warm tortillas, fresh linens, and rose perfume. Then I gave my *abuelito* a big kiss on his wrinkled cheek.

Behind them a parade of family streamed from the sprawling adobe and red tile house, hugging and kissing. We're big on that. Altogether there were eighteen of us, plus Abuelita's housekeeper, Esperanza.

We spent our holiday just like every year—talking, eating, and arguing. The men played dominoes and bickered over politics. The women made tamales and gossiped about families. We kids played games, fought over TV channels to watch, laughed, screamed, and built a *Nacimiento*. (Nativity scene).

Every morning for breakfast we ate *bolillos* of warm bread and melted butter, with eggs and Esperanza's best-in-the-world hot chocolate. We usually didn't eat lunch till two, after which everyone rested with a *siesta*.

At dusk each night the entire family went caroling in candlelit *posadas*, pretending to be looking for lodging in Bethlehem.

Next day, our routine started over, till *Noche Buena*

(Christmas Eve), which in our family was like a major fashion show. Everybody dressed up in their very finest for midnight mass.

Then during communion our *tíos* snuck home. By the time we kids returned, a baby Jesus figurine had dramatically appeared in the *Nacimiento* cradle. Alongside him mountains of presents were stacked. Everyone stayed up till dawn, opening and trying out gifts, eating, drinking, lighting sparklers, and setting off fireworks.

It was after ten the next morning before I woke up. Bleary-eyed, I climbed over snoring guests, stumbling toward the smell of hot chocolate and the arguing voices of Mami, Abuelita, and Tía Lupe.

Lupe (Mami's older sister) is tall, wiry, and totally bossy. She's forever telling Mami what to do, and at least once during every visit they get into a fight. Apparently today was the day.

"Again you're meddling in something that's none of your business!" Mami snapped at Lupe as I stepped into the kitchen.

"Yes, it is my business," Lupe shot back. "When the phone wakes me at seven Christmas morning, it becomes my business."

"I don't want him calling here," Abuelita complained in an upset tone.

The three of them clattered dishes from last night's mess while Esperanza, seeing me, cleared a corner of the kitchen table.

"What happened?" I asked her in a low voice as she set before me a cup of steaming chocolate.

"You'd better stay out of it," Esperanza whispered. "Your papá called to say *Feliz Navidad* and woke your aunt up."

"He's as inconsiderate as ever," Lupe told Mami as she scraped leftovers into the trash. "I told you not to marry him."

It bothered me to hear her attacking Papi. Yeah, he *is* thoughtless sometimes, but who was Lupe to judge? No way could I stay out of this.

"Everybody's inconsiderate sometimes," I cut in.

"Yes." Lupe glared at me, bags under her eyes. "Especially your papá."

"Enough!" Mami jumped in. "He's still her father. I don't like you talking that way in front of her."

Lupe's husband, Tío Fausto, walked in just then, stretching, yawning and scratching his big stomach. "What's going on, *mi amor*?" He pecked Lupe a kiss. "If you want to wake the whole house, better to do it singing." (That's another Spanish saying.)

Lupe rolled her eyes at him and turned away, rattling more dishes, certain to wake everyone still sleeping. And I burned my tongue on the hot chocolate, probably because I was so upset. The burn kept me thinking of Papi during the whole rest of the day.

Later, when I was helping Abuelita cut flowers in the garden, I asked her, "Why don't you like Papi?"

"Because he hurt your mamá very deeply." Abuelita snipped some snapdragons with her clippers. "She adored your papá, and he broke her heart."

After Abuelita took the flowers inside I stayed in the garden, sitting in the sun and wondering if Mami's heart would stay broken and closed or if . . .

I hoped Rodolfo would call her. She hadn't talked to him since we'd left home. (I knew because I'd asked.)

I spent most of the rest of my time with my favorite cousin, Elisa, who's fifteen. She and I tried on and swapped clothes we'd gotten for Christmas. (We're the same size, except her boobs are bigger. I hate that.) We burned a killer CD of our favorite Latin groups. We gave each other head-to-toe salt scrubs and made facial masks from mashed strawberries and cornstarch. We were getting along so perfectly . . . till I showed her the party photo of Frederick and me for the millionth time.

"*Que chulo!*" She grinned at the picture. "He's so cute! You know who he looks like? That singer. Know the one I mean? The gay guy in that band."

Suddenly, my body tensed. "Frederick's *not* gay." I

snatched the photo out of her hands.

"*Qué te pasa?*" She backed up, studying me with a puzzled look. "I didn't say he was. All I said was he's cute. What's your problem?"

I glanced down at Frederick's photo, not sure why I'd jumped on Elisa's case. I guess I felt kind of touchy after the whole episode with Carmen asking Frederick if he was gay.

"Just because a boy is cute," I said to Elisa, "doesn't mean he's gay. I told you Frederick and I kissed. We make out all the time."

It was a slight exaggeration, but the point was: If Frederick was gay, he wouldn't have kissed me, would he?

Elisa shrugged. "Whatever."

Maybe she and I were starting to get on each other's nerves. I felt bad for snapping at her. "You want to go shopping?" I asked.

"No, thanks." Her voice was cool. "I promised Laura I'd call her." (Laura was Elisa's best friend.) A minute later I'd been ditched by my favorite cousin.

I sat on the bed by myself, staring at the photo of Frederick, wondering: *What singer in what band had Elisa meant?* I didn't know of any gay singers. Then I started wondering, *What makes a guy gay? Are they born that way? Do they hate girls?*

I'd never actually met anyone gay, unless you

counted Iggy. But was he really gay or did people just say that? Either way I didn't like how people picked on him. So what if he was gay? He didn't hurt anyone.

I went to see what my other cousins were doing. They were all glued to the TV watching that cartoon about the ogre.

"Haven't you guys seen this a thousand times already?" I asked, but they ignored me.

It sucked having only one girl cousin close to my age. I missed my friends and wished I was with them. I'd been meaning to get them each a souvenir gift with my Christmas money and decided, *Why not do it now?*

I walked around the knickknack shops and stands of Tlaquepaque square and found a little clay candle dish for María. She loves candles. For Nora I found a beautiful woven bookmark of multicolored threads. For José I decided on a leather belt. They have *the* best leather in Mexico. For Carmen I got a cool papier-mâché figure that was either an angel with horns or a devil with wings. And I decided to get one for Elisa too, to apologize.

I also wanted to buy Frederick a little something, but wasn't sure what to get him. Shopping for a guy is lots harder. I looked at sparkly embroidered vests, Rolex watches ("Guaranteed authentic." Yeah, sure), and colorful *charro* hats. But nothing seemed right.

Then I passed beneath an archway off the main square where an old Indian woman sat in the shadows, polishing silver jewelry spread on her blanket. Amid the earrings and bracelets, I saw it . . . a silver neck chain sparkling beneath a shaft of sunlight.

*"Hola, linda."* The old woman smiled at me, her weathered face crinkling.

*"Buenas tardes, señora."* I leaned over, picking up the necklace, and ran my fingers across the smooth metal. "How much does it cost?"

Even though silver is cheaper in Mexico, the woman's price was for way more money than I had. Of course, you're supposed to haggle with street vendors. Only the clueless tourists pay full price. But I always felt greedy haggling.

I mean, you could tell by the old lady's faded dress she wasn't rich. Yet at the same time, I'd already spent half my money on presents for the Sexies and Elisa. I really didn't have enough left for what she was asking.

I gently returned the necklace to the blanket. "I'm sorry," I told the woman and started to walk away.

*"Niña!"* The woman waved me back, picking up the necklace. "Because you're so pretty I'll give it to you for half price. Try it on. Let's see how beautiful you look."

"Oh, it's not for me," I told her. And even at half price I still didn't have enough money. "I'm sorry, but thank you anyway." Once again I started to walk off.

"*Linda!*" Again the woman motioned me back, cutting the price a third time.

"I'm really very sorry, *señora,* but I still don't have enough money."

Her smile turned into a scowl. "Well, then, how much money do you have?"

A little embarrassed, I emptied my wallet into my hand, counting the bills and coins. No way would she possibly let me have it for what I could offer, would she?

"*Ay, no!*" The old woman turned her nose up.

Disappointed, I returned the money to my wallet. "I'm sorry," I said again.

"Is it for your boyfriend?" the woman asked, her face softening.

"Yes," I replied, even though Frederick wasn't officially my boyfriend. Yet.

"*Bueno.*" She slid the neck chain into a little plastic bag for me. "But only because it's for your boyfriend."

Was she serious? I quickly emptied my wallet and clasped her hands, unable to believe my luck. I ran home, arriving out of breath, and found Mami in the garden playing croquet with Stevie and some cousins.

"Look what I got Frederick!" I showed Mami the neck chain.

"That's very beautiful." She admired it and raised an eyebrow. "Are you sure you want to give him something that expensive?"

"It didn't cost that much." I explained to her about the woman lowering the price.

Then I went to give Elisa the angel/devil I'd brought her. She loved it.

After that we got along great for the rest of the visit, though I never again brought up Frederick.

On New Year's Eve, as dusk approached, the boys began setting off firecrackers and the adults began drinking rum punch. Elisa and I also tried some. She liked it, but I didn't. As midnight approached we all began watching the countdown on TV. Ten minutes before midnight, the phone rang. Esperanza answered and motioned for Mami.

"Who is it?" Mami asked as she hurried to the phone, smoothing her hair.

"A *señor* named Rodolfo," Esperanza said and Mami's face lit up.

At the stroke of twelve, she was still talking to him.

As I exchanged hugs and kisses with my cousins, *abuelitos,* and even Tía Lupe, I wished I could've talked to Frederick too, but I didn't even have his phone number in Wisconsin.

About one o'clock I went to my room. After climbing into bed I pulled out the party photo of Frederick and me, staring at it. Then . . . Can I actually admit this? I kissed it. I know that was lame, but . . . I missed him.

# Chapter 16

## Frederick

I'd promised myself that when I boarded the plane for Wisconsin, I'd leave behind all my confusion about my closet kiss with Xio—and what (or who) I'd been thinking about while kissing her.

San Cayetano's red hills and canyons became smaller and smaller beneath the plane window, and after four long hours our flight began its descent toward the snow-covered landscape surrounding Minneapolis.

Stepping out of the airport terminal I put on my winter coat. For the first time since we'd moved to California I was freezing.

During the drive in our rental car to Eau Claire, Mom cell-phoned Grandma Kate (my dad's mom) and said we were on our way. After she hung up I called Janice.

"Hi!" I shouted when she answered. "Guess where I am?"

Janice screamed with excitement, "William's here too!" He picked up the other extension. "Hey, California dude."

As the three of us talked I shifted in the velour seat, hardly able to sit still. The hour and a half drive seemed to take forever.

My Grandma Kate lives only a few blocks from the house where we used to live. (My Grandpa Carl died five years ago.) It was great to see her again, especially since we hadn't come home for Thanksgiving.

She fixed us cheddar, tomato, and mayo sandwiches. I gobbled down a couple and told her about our new house and my new school. Then I helped Dad unload the car and told Mom I was going to see Janice and William.

"But, honey, you just got here."

"I know, but I haven't seen them in months." I tore out toward Janice's, taking the route by my old house—just for old times' sake. Maybe I'd even say hi to the new people living there.

But as I hurried down the snow-packed street and our old place came into view, my pace slowed. I stared openmouthed in disbelief, my breath steaming in the cold.

Our once beautiful ecru-colored house with walnut trim was now painted vomit green and puky yellow. On the lawn, tacky garden gnomes poked out of the snow. A tattered _EASON'S G_EETINGS banner hung from the awning.

Could this possibly be the same house I'd grown up in? What the heck had the new people done? Were they on drugs? I wanted to bang on the door and tell them "Get out!"

Instead I shoved my gloved fists into my jacket pockets and continued trudging toward Janice's.

When she answered the door the first thing I noticed was her form-fitting pink sweater, beneath which bulged her, um . . . breasts.

Where had they come from? I mean, I knew where they'd come from. But they weren't there when I'd left Wisconsin four months ago—at least not like they were now, squishing against my chest as she wrapped her arms around me.

Behind her stood William, even taller than when I'd last seen him. Was I the only one still the same?

"You're so tanned!" Janice exclaimed, unsquishing me.

That was definitely true. In comparison everyone here looked so white.

"Hey, dude." William waved and smiled. I expected him to wrap his arm around me like Victor did, but I had to remember guys didn't do that with each other here.

Janice's mom and dad said hi and asked all sorts

of questions about California—how was the weather, if I'd seen any movie stars, that sort of stuff.

Then Janice, William, and I hung out on the carpet in her room, catching up on all the stuff we hadn't IM'd each other during the past few months. It was great being back together in person.

Except something else seemed different about Janice and William besides how they looked. There was a change between them—something that hadn't come through over the Net. They weren't picking on each other like they used to.

"Tell us more about your friends in California," Janice said.

I told them about everyone and brought out the photos from Xio's party.

"She's pretty!" Janice pointed at Xio and studied me. "Has she become your girlfriend?"

I felt myself grow warm beneath my collar. How should I answer that? Xio and I had kissed, hadn't we? Yeah, but . . . "I wouldn't exactly say she's my girlfriend."

"I bet she *is*," Janice insisted. "Isn't she? Come on, admit it."

I tugged at my collar. "Maybe," I finally said, hoping Janice would ease up. "I guess so."

"Way to go, dude." William punched my shoulder. "She's hot!"

"Hey!" Janice gave him a swat on the arm. Then she turned to me and whispered, "Did you know Marcie has a boyfriend now?"

"No way!" I whispered back. "Bookworm Marcie?"

"Why are you two whispering?" William laughed. "You think she's under the bed listening?"

Janice ignored him. "Guess who her boyfriend is. Jim Jorgensen."

"Jimmy Jorgensen?" I exclaimed. Jimmy had always been a jock—totally into sports, even in grade school—not someone I would've imagined paired up with Marcie.

"He goes by 'Jim' now," Janice said. "They're meeting us at the mall. Marcie is dying to see you."

Janice's mom called us downstairs for some cheese and crackers. Then Janice, William, and I headed toward the mall.

As we walked down the street a salt truck rumbled up behind us—a sound I hadn't heard for ages.

I noticed William put his arm around Janice's shoulder, nudging her out of the street. Once the truck had passed his arm remained there, and Janice wrapped hers around his waist.

Like a chucked snowball, it suddenly struck me what was different about the two of them. My best Wisconsin friends were now boyfriend and girlfriend. I stood dazed for a moment, absorbing the impact of that realization.

At the mall food court, Marcie was waiting with Jimmy—I mean *Jim*—Jorgensen. It was great to see Marcie again and ask her what she'd been reading. She's always been so into sci-fi. I loved to hear her describe the plots and characters.

But Jim only wanted to talk about sports. "So do you surf?" he asked me. "What's it like?"

"I haven't tried it yet. Not everyone in California surfs."

"Oh," he said. "I've heard it's supposed to be like snowboarding. How about skin diving? Have you tried that?"

"No, but I play soccer." At least I could tell him about that.

All of them asked me questions as the five of us wandered around the mall, talking and joking. It felt great being the center of attention and being back together with my friends, even though I hadn't counted on the addition of Jim.

It was weird watching him hold hands with Marcie—and William hold hands with Janice. But they seemed happy. Why hadn't I felt happy like that holding hands with Xio?

As we walked through the mall Jim abruptly

muttered to the rest of us, "Fag alert!"

Ahead of us two men in jeans and designer jackets pointed in a store window, discussing clothes. They looked nice enough. How could Jim tell they were gay? And why did he care if they were?

I would've asked Jim that, but what if he challenged me in return? I imagined Janice, William, and Marcie eyeing me as if I was some sort of freak—just like they were staring at these two guys.

Janice cupped her hand over her mouth and whispered to us, "Last week I saw a couple of them here in the mall actually holding hands."

"No way!" William said.

"Barf!" Jim made a face.

"Really?" I asked.

Then Marcie piped up as if to top Janice. "I saw an episode of the *The Real World* where they showed two guys *kissing*."

*When was that?* I wondered. The times I'd watched *TRW* they'd only showed stuff like fork throwing.

"Two guys?" Jim stuck a finger down his throat as if vomiting.

"You shouldn't judge other people," Marcie scolded back at him.

"Yeah," I agreed, a little emboldened. And in my mind I wondered, *What would it be like to actually see two guys kiss?* Maybe I should start watching *TRW* more often.

Christmas Day all my relatives came to gather at Grandma's. It sort of made up for Thanksgiving. I helped her make our prize-winning cranberry-orange relish, and she saved the turkey wishbone for her and me to break.

If I ended up with the big half I already knew what I'd wish for.

*Please God, don't let me be gay. I'm weird enough as it is.*

Christmas evening I stopped by Marcie's, Janice's, and William's, exchanging gifts.

While shopping I'd also looked for a present to take back to Xio, but I couldn't decide what to get her. I wanted to find something really special but . . . would she think I was being romantic?

I decided I should try talking to William about the whole Xio thing. Maybe he could help me sort out my mixed-up feelings.

One afternoon he and I hung out in his room, lying on the carpet. We watched a DVD movie in which aliens snatched the bodies of humans and replaced them with alien look-alikes.

"Can I ask you a question?" I said during one of the guy-girl scenes. "Have you and Janice like, um, kissed?"

"Yeah." He turned to me, smiling goofily, and punched my arm. "See what happens when you move away?"

I laughed, socked him back, and thought about my party kiss with Xio—and what had happened. William and I watched the movie some more, then I asked, "When you kiss Janice . . . do you ever think of someone else?"

William's face scrunched up as if puzzled. "You mean like babes?"

I stared back at him. Had my best friend from grade school actually used the word *babes*? He never used to even notice girls. Now he was kissing and calling them *babes*? Who was this new William? And what had happened with my old friend William?

"Um, not exactly babes," I responded. "Just . . . other people."

"Hmn." William thought about it a minute, then shook his head. "No. Why? Do you?"

My throat tightened around my voice. "No," I lied.

He gave me a curious look. I lowered my gaze, thinking I must sound like a nutcase. But how could I tell him how mixed-up I felt inside—how I'd thought about Victor when I was kissing Xio, how I'd looked up *gay* on the Internet, how I feared I might be weirder than I'd ever thought.

"Speaking of kissing," William said, "have you

kissed . . . what did you say her name was?"

"Xio?" I replied, my ears burning red. "Yeah, um, we've kissed."

"I figured you had." William laughed and punched me again. "Isn't she hot?"

I hesitated. Although I'd always thought Xio was beautiful, I knew there was a difference between thinking a girl was beautiful and finding her hot.

"She's really nice, but . . . I'm not sure I like her *that* way—you know—as a girlfriend?"

William studied me a minute, then turned to watch the aliens snatch another body. "Bummer," he said.

"Yeah," I agreed.

For New Year's Eve, Marcie invited me to a party at her house, but I'd come down with a sore throat so I didn't go. It was probably just as well, since at midnight everybody probably would've paired up kissing—everyone except me.

I slept late the next morning and mostly stayed in bed, thinking how much things had changed since I'd moved.

The night before we were to return to California I told Mom I was going out for a while.

"But, honey," she protested. "You're still sick. Where are you going?"

"Just for a walk. That's all. I'll be back soon."

She insisted I bundle up in a million layers, then I tramped down the quiet snow-packed street, back toward our old house. The place didn't look quite so gross in the dark. Behind the gauze living room curtains a blue glow hinted at a TV.

To the right of that, the blinds were lowered in my old room. But I could still see the layout clearly in my mind—where I used to play video games with William, read sci-fi stories with Marcie, watch TV with Janice . . .

Why had we had to move? Why did everything have to change?

A light snow started falling. As flakes drifted gently onto my cheeks, I wiped my face and tramped back down the street.

# Chapter 17

## Xio

Although I'm proud to be American, each time I leave Mexico I bawl like a baby, guaranteed. It's weird how a place can have such a pull on you.

Yet once we arrived home I was ecstatic to be back in my own room again, with all my stuff and able to phone my friends.

I immediately checked phone messages. There were about a million from Carmen, upset about Victor. As soon as I called her she rushed over. Her eyes were puffy like she'd been crying, but her gaze was more angry than sad.

She described how over the holidays she'd spied Victor holding hands with some high schooler at the mall. But she hadn't let them see her.

"I hate him!" Carmen yanked Victor's photo from her wallet and ripped it apart, cursing the entire time. When Carmen gets *furiosa* her mouth becomes a total sewer. I quickly closed my bedroom door and turned up the music so no one would hear.

"The *sin vergüenza*," I agreed. (Literally that means he's without shame—kind of like calling him a slime ball.)

Carmen abruptly stopped ranting, shooting me a pained look. "He's not *that* bad."

Was she actually defending him? "Carmen, you just said you saw him holding hands—"

"I know," Carmen interrupted, "but the girl probably put the moves on him first."

I sat speechless, my jaw clamped shut. Did Carmen truly believe Victor had been the helpless victim of some high school man-eater? Oh, right. Poor defenseless Victor, too weak to keep a big, bad girl from holding his hand.

I wanted to shake some sense into Carmen except I saw her eyes turning shiny and her lip start quivering. The next instant she burst into sobs, her arms encircling me.

Gently I patted her back, rocking her. Even though I was ticked off about Victor I held my tongue, thinking how Carmen's such a Scorpio. She may try to come off as tough and independent, but beneath that crusty shell she's as mushy as you can get.

The thing is though, she won't let people see that tender side of her—except at times like now. I think I'm the only person she ever cries with. Maybe if she did let Victor see that side of her, he wouldn't be such a jerk.

When Carmen finally stopped bawling I asked, "Did you tell Victor you saw him with that girl?"

"No way!" Carmen walked to my dresser mirror and wiped her eyes. "Are you crazy? That would be so humiliating."

"Well, then . . . Does he even know you're angry?"

"He should! When he phoned I cussed him out and hung up on him."

"But you didn't tell him why you're angry?"

"He can figure it out. He's not stupid. He knows what he did."

"Carmen!" I shook my head. "You should at least explain to him why you're angry."

Carmen pursed her lips as if thinking about it. "No," she said at last and crouched on the floor, picking up the scraps of Victor's picture. "I don't want to talk about it anymore. Do you have some tape?"

I watched her, wondering: *What is it about love that makes people so weird?* Grudgingly I brought Carmen a roll of tape, and she pieced the creep's photo back together.

Eager to change the subject, I gave her the souvenir angel/devil I'd brought her.

"Thanks, Xio." She squeezed me in a hug. "I know I can always count on you."

Yeah, yeah, whatever. If she only knew how annoyed I got with her sometimes. Nevertheless I hugged her back. After all, just because I got miffed didn't mean I don't love her.

After she left I spent the rest of the evening on the phone with the other Sexies, catching up on everyone's drama.

José told how during her visit to Tijuana some guy tried to pick her pocket. She smacked him harder than she meant to and his nose started bleeding as he ran away. Ever since she'd felt guilty about it, wondering if she'd overreacted.

"Excuse me!" I protested. "But didn't he try to rob you? Maybe he'll think twice next time."

Next came Nora's tragedy. Even though her visit with her dad went better this time, when she got home her hard drive had crashed. Her ten-page paper on the forced repatriation of Mexican-Americans during the Great Depression had been wiped out.

"Now I have to write the whole thing over again."

I felt so bad for her. "I'll help you," I offered, although I really didn't know what I could do.

As for María, at least there had been no fight between her mom and Tito. Instead her crisis was that Gordo had been phoning ever since their closet kiss.

"*Ay, Díos ayudame.* I don't know what to say. What am I going to do?"

I tried to help her figure out what she wanted to do, but by the end of the call she was still a bundle of nerves.

Compared to my friends' calamities, my holiday seemed totally boring.

Later that evening Frederick phoned. I'd called him that afternoon and left a message. Now I told him all about my trip. "I wish you could come with me sometime and meet my *abuelitos.* I'd show you around. We'd have so much fun."

Then I caught him up on the Sexies, including Carmen's fight—if you could call it that—with Victor.

"But don't tell Victor about it, okay?" I didn't want Frederick and me caught in the middle between Victor and Carmen.

"Can you come over tomorrow?" I asked. "I brought you something I want to give you."

"Sure. What is it?"

"Just a little something," I said. "Now, tell me about your trip to Wisconsin."

Before going to bed I asked Mami, "Do you have a box and wrapping paper I can use for Frederick's necklace?"

We rummaged through drawers and found a hinged velvet watch case that was perfect. After wrapping the silver chain, I stored the box in my nightstand drawer. Then I lay down in my very own bed for the first time in ages.

Sunday afternoon when the doorbell rang I sprang through the living room, brushing past Stevie. "I'll get it!"

On the front stoop with his hands in his pockets stood Frederick. *"Hola,"* he said, smiling and sniffling.

Without even thinking, I threw my arms around him. "Hi!"

"Um, you'd better not get too close. I'm getting over a sore throat."

*"Ay, mi pobrecito!"* I pulled his hand from his pocket and led him across the living room, where Mami was on the phone with Rodolfo.

"Hi, Frederick," she said, covering the phone. "How was Wisconsin?"

"Cold," Frederick said, giving a little cough.

"We're going to my room," I told Mami.

She raised an eyebrow and told me, *"Deja la puerta abierta, por favor,"* which means "Leave the door open, please."

*"Ay, Mami!"* I complained. I'd been wondering if she'd say anything, since I'd never had a boy in my

room before. (I mean a *boyfriend*-type boy.)

"Xiomara!" she said. She hardly ever uses my full name.

I ignored her, leading Frederick to my room, while debating whether to leave the door open or close it defiantly. I hate when Mami gets so overprotective. Just because I wanted a little privacy, did she think I was going to throw myself at Frederick? I decided to leave the door open only a hairline crack—so no pathetically old-fashioned mom or snoopy little brother could peer in.

"You've got a lot of pillows." Frederick stood in the center of the room, sniffling and looking around.

"Yeah. You want a tissue?" I pulled one from my nightstand box.

"Huh? Sure. Thanks." Frederick dabbed his nose and glanced at my Little Mermaid lamp. "That was my favorite Disney movie when I was little. I never knew they made a lamp of it."

"Well, it's pretty old. I'm kind of over it. My dad gave it to me." I sat down on the bed and turned on the lamp so Frederick could see the fish on the shade light up.

"It used to have a clock there." I pointed to the empty space beneath Ariel's tail. "But it broke and they don't make them anymore."

"You sure?" Frederick asked. He was still standing in the center of my room, hands in his pockets. Even with a cold, he looked adorable.

"Yeah." I patted the bedspread next to me. "Come sit. I want to give you something."

He peered at the spot my hand touched as if it was booby-trapped. I smiled to reassure him. He shuffled over and scooted onto the bed beside me. I opened the nightstand drawer and handed him the brightly wrapped box.

"Xio, you shouldn't have." He glanced at me, then at the box, then at me again.

So close beside me his eyes seemed more brilliantly blue than ever, and I felt the thousand butterfly wings brushing me all over again.

Frederick pulled the tissue from his pocket and wiped his nose. "Should I open it?"

"Well, duh." I grinned.

He tore off the wrapping and opened the velvet-covered box, his pupils growing wide. "Xio!" He gulped and his Adam's apple bobbed up and down.

"I thought of you the instant I saw it." I scooted across the bed closer to him. "You like it?"

"Yeah, it's beautiful." As he stared at the chain I pulled my hair away from my face—in case he decided to lean over and kiss me.

But when he glanced at me his face became tense, as if something was bothering him.

"Is something wrong?" I asked nervously.

"No. . . ." He bit into his bottom lip as if too shy to tell me something and stared into my eyes. I was certain he was about to press his tender lips to mine.

"Never mind." He let out a huge sigh. "It's beautiful."

Then why didn't he kiss me? His shyness was totally getting on my nerves. Maybe he was concerned about his sniffles. Well, then I'd have to make the move . . .

"Why don't you try it on?" I told him.

He peered across the room into my dresser mirror and lifted the chain, clasping it around his neck. I gazed alongside him, leaning into his warm shoulder. "You look great."

He turned to me, his lips just inches from mine, and I opened my mouth to—

The door squeaked, revealing my snoopy little brother's eyeballs.

"Stevie!" I screamed as his footsteps trotted away on the hallway carpet. I was about to leap off the bed to slam the door, but just then Mami opened it.

"Come have some cookies." Her eyes flashed

between Frederick and me as if she'd just busted us. If only!

Nevertheless Frederick sprang off the bed, blushing as if we *had* done something.

In the kitchen Mami served Stevie and us some *cajeta* we'd brought back from Mexico. While Frederick enjoyed the thick, sugary milk spread on María cookies, I steamed with anger at both Stevie and Mami, but mostly Mami.

After Frederick left I charged back to the kitchen and let her have it.

"Why do you want to ruin my life? Why can't you just trust me for one single second? You think just because I have a boy in my room I'm going to get pregnant or something? Well, you're not going to keep me locked up my whole life. I'm not going to wait around forever to end up with a cold, shriveled heart like you!"

Mami winced as if I'd stabbed her with a knife. I couldn't believe I'd just said what I did. My voice broke and I stormed from the kitchen, nearly knocking Stevie over.

I slammed the door to my room and flung myself on the bed. When would I learn to keep my big mouth shut? I loved Mami too much to hurt her like that. But why couldn't she trust me? Couldn't she understand that just because I wanted to kiss a boy didn't mean I was going to do something stupid?

Half of me thought I knew everything. But the other half of me believed I wouldn't ever know anything at all.

# Chapter 18

## Frederick

When I got home from Xio's, Mom noticed the necklace right away.

"Honey, that's beautiful." She ran her fingers along the chain, giving me one of those goofy parent smiles. "Xio must like you a lot."

Oh, brother. Just what I didn't want to hear.

I went up to my room and lay down on my bed, staring at the ceiling. Then I got up again and peered into the mirror at the gleaming necklace.

The gift had been really nice of Xio. She was a great friend—funny, sweet, thoughtful, generous. . . . So why didn't I like her as anything more?

I wished I'd been able to find her a present. I'd actually gotten an idea for what to get when I'd been at her place. I could probably find it on the Web. But would she understand the gift was meant *only* as a friend? Or would it only further confuse things?

* * *

At lunch on Monday Xio's friends fussed and cooed over the necklace as though it were made of diamonds. Xio looked on proudly. Even Carmen cheered up from her falling-out with Victor—for a moment. Then she began bad-mouthing him again.

"He's a skank." Carmen glared across the lunchroom at Victor, who was joking with the other guys.

"Look at him playing *inocente*. This morning he told me hi as though nothing was wrong."

"You should tell him why you're angry," Nora said.

"If you're not going to," José agreed, "then *I'll* tell him."

"Tell him whatever you want." Carmen thrust out her jaw, continuing to watch Victor. "I don't want anything more to do with the jerk."

I could understand her being mad and jealous about Victor holding another girl's hand. I would be too if I were her. But it was hard to hear her talk so bad about him.

When I saw Victor at soccer, I didn't repeat any of the stuff Carmen had said. I figured why get mixed up in it? Besides, as the week went by I'd begun to realize it wasn't totally a bad thing Victor and Carmen had fought. Now Victor was no longer pulled away by her after soccer. Instead he stayed around with the other guys and me, joking and hanging out.

Friday afternoon when everyone was finally heading home, Victor asked, "Hey, Rico, you want to come over?"

"Sure!" I nearly shouted from excitement. It marked the first time Victor had ever invited me to his house.

We walked in the direction of the mall, talking about what we'd done over the holidays, the presents we'd gotten and movies we'd seen. He didn't mention anything about the girl at the mall. Finally we turned down a street of older wooden houses with sagging porches.

Victor led me up the driveway of a squat bungalow and gently patted the fender of an old pickup truck perched on concrete blocks. "How do you like my baby? My dad gave her to me. You know what FORD stands for?"

"No." I shook my head.

"Found On Road Dead." He punched me, chuckling. "I'm bringing her back to life for when I get my license."

At the back of the house he pulled open the screen door and led me into the kitchen, saying, *"Mi casa es tu casa."*

The room had a sweet smell of onions, garlic, and peppers. From a TV in the living room came Spanish voices.

"Come meet my granddad," Victor said, leading me through an archway. In a chair facing close to the TV sat a skinny old man in a white shirt, linen pants, and slippers.

"*Abuelito,*" Victor called. "*Este es mi amigo, Federico.*"

"*Mucho gusto,*" I said, like Xio had taught me—Spanish for "nice to meet you."

"*Es un güerito,*" his granddad told Victor and put his hand out for me to shake.

As I took the soft bony hand, I whispered to Victor, "What did he say?"

"*Güerito,*" Victor said. "*Güero* means, like, blond white dude." While Victor spoke, his granddad reached his hand up, his old quivering fingertips tapping my hair.

"Why's he touching my head?"

"I don't know. He's kind of senile—you know—Alzheimery." Victor picked up a tube of hand lotion from the lamp table and pulled his granddad's hand away from my head. "His skin gets really dry. He loves having lotion rubbed on."

As Victor massaged cream into his granddad's hands, I gazed around the room. Whereas Xio's house looked typically American, Victor's looked like the homes of Mexican families in movies, with a Virgin of Guadalupe statue in the corner, a round

Aztec calendar on the wall, wrought iron candle-holders, stuff like that.

"Want some?" Victor squirted some lotion on my hands. His granddad had closed his eyes, his lids fluttering, and his head folded over, asleep.

"I'm hungry." Victor nudged me back toward the kitchen. "You want something to eat?"

We grabbed a couple of sodas and a bag of *pan dulce* and carried them down the narrow hall. Victor pressed me with his shoulder, laughing, as he squeezed me up against the wall, but I pushed him back. Then Victor swung his arm around me and picked me up, carried me into his room, and tossed me onto his unmade bed, both of us cracking up the whole time.

The walls of the small room were plastered with posters—of racing cars, soccer players, megaboobed young women, and a poster of a good-looking Latino baseball player.

Victor saw me looking at the guy. "Next week we'll switch to softball in the afternoons. Do you play?"

"Yeah," I told him. Even though I'd actually only played softball in PE, I figured playing catcher would be like playing goalie.

Victor dropped his backpack to the floor and bounced onto the bed beside me. He yanked off his tennis shoes, filling the room with their Victor smell—not a bad smell, at least not to me. He tossed the shoes across the cluttered room and told me, "Take yours off too. Want to play *GTA*?"

"Sure." I pulled my shoes off and placed them neatly in a corner.

Victor grabbed a controller from the shelves crammed with a PlayStation console, TV, DVD player, and cologne bottles. For the rest of the afternoon we played *Grand Theft Auto*, ate *pan dulce*, and laughed like loonies, till Victor's mom came to the door.

"Hi, Mom," Victor called over his shoulder from the controller. "This is Frederick."

Even if Victor hadn't said she was his mom, I could've guessed it. With her dark hair and eyes, she was beautiful.

I jumped up, suddenly realizing I hadn't let my own mom know where I was. "Hi, Mrs. Carrera. Can I use your phone? I forgot to call my mom."

"Tell your mom you want to stay for dinner!" Victor shouted as Mrs. Carrera led me to the phone. I decided to try my mom's work number first, hoping she'd still be there.

When she answered I let out a sigh of relief. "Hi, Mom. I'm at my friend Victor's from soccer. I'm going to stay for dinner, okay?"

First she made me answer a million questions:

"Where does Victor live? What's his phone number? Who's home with you two?"

You would've thought I'd been kidnapped or something. But finally she said yes.

Soon the smell of boiling rice was wafting from the kitchen and Mrs. Carrera called, "Victor! Come set the table!"

While Victor poured drinks I watched his mom prepare our steaks—rubbing them with lime juice, adding garlic and pepper, then searing them. They came out delicious, along with the rice, beans, and tortillas.

Victor cut his granddad's steak into tiny pieces for him and Mrs. Carrera asked me the usual parent questions: "Do you have any brothers and sisters? What do your mom and dad do for work? What's your favorite subject in school?"

After helping clean up Victor and I returned to his room, where he told me to pick out a DVD. I chose a Batman movie I like a lot.

While Victor inserted the disk, I pointed to a photo on the dresser of a mustached man. "Is that your dad?"

"Yeah." Victor plopped onto the bed beside me and leaned back on the pillows. "They split up two years ago."

"Do you see him much?"

"On Saturdays I help him out. He has his own garage. Then I spend the night at his place." Victor gazed at the TV. "Hey, watch this. The opening's the best part."

He tugged my shoulder, pulling me back on the bed, so we lay side by side. Occasionally he'd yell out comments at the screen: "Don't do it!" "Watch out!" "You dummy." "Smack him!" "Yeah!"

When he'd done the same thing during previews at the movie with Xio, the girls had shushed him. Tonight without them around, he sometimes got so excited he wrapped his arm around my neck or socked my thigh. I didn't mind. I thought it was funny.

As we watched the movie I imagined what it would be to like to live with your best friend, like Batman did with Robin, in some huge place like stately Wayne Manor. Except I'd definitely redesign the place to brighten it up.

When the movie neared the end, Mrs. Carrera appeared at the doorway. "It's getting late, boys. Victor, help your *abuelito* to bed."

"Frederick's spending the night!" Victor announced.

That was the first I'd heard of it. "For real?" I asked.

"Yeah." Victor nodded. "Want to?"

"Sure," I said, trying to keep my voice steady. "But I'd better tell my mom."

I hoped she wouldn't ask a bazillion questions again. In Wisconsin William and I had spent the night lots of times. No big deal, as long as it was a Saturday or even Friday, like tonight. But since this was my first time at Victor's, my mom became a total worrywart. "Why didn't you ask me earlier? How can I be sure you'll be safe? Let me speak to Victor's mom."

I called Mrs. Carrera and stood by listening while they talked.

Fortunately they got along right away. When Mrs. Carrera passed the phone back to me, my mom proclaimed, "She sounds very nice."

"Mom, what did you expect? Can I stay?"

"Yes," Mom said. "Oh, by the way, Xio phoned. She asked for you to call her."

"Okay," I agreed. But as soon as I hung up Victor's mom said, "You boys take a shower before you go to bed," and I totally forgot about Xio.

"You shower first," Victor told me. "But you better leave me some hot water."

No problem there. I turned the water on to freezing, hoping to calm the excitement I was feeling. By the time I finished showering, my skin was spiked with goose bumps.

I'd asked Victor if I could borrow some pajamas, but he didn't wear pj's, so he loaned me a pair of sweats that smelled like his brown sugar cologne. Only problem was the large-size shirt hung down to my knees and the pants bunched up around my ankles.

"Is that you in there?" Victor kidded me as I padded into the bedroom.

While he showered I tried to figure out where to stack my folded clothes. There wasn't anyplace amid the shoes, *pan dulce* wrappers, books, empty soft drink cans, soccer balls, and video game cartridges.

So I began to tidy up the room. I folded his clothes, replaced CDs in their cases, and tossed trash into the wastebasket. Within minutes the place looked a thousand times better.

"Hey!" Victor laughed. "Why'd you mess up my room?"

I turned to see him standing in only his boxer shorts, while he rubbed his hair with a towel. His bare chest sparkled with water droplets, glistening down the six little bricks of his abs.

I'm not sure why I stared at him. It wasn't like I'd never seen a guy in shorts before. Except this felt different. My skin was tingling all over. And my heart pounded furiously.

Victor shook his wet hair onto me.

"Hey, stop!" I shielded my face from the water. But he grabbed my wrists, pressing me onto the bed, sprinkling me with wet drops as I laughed beneath him.

When he finally let go, I wiped my cheeks with a baggy sweatshirt sleeve and he pulled a sleeping bag from the closet.

"You take my bed," he told me. "I'll sleep on the floor."

"I don't mind the floor," I protested, but Victor wouldn't hear of it. He unrolled the sleeping bag onto the narrow stretch of floor, grabbed one of the pillows from the bed, and crawled into the bag's plaid interior.

In turn, I slid beneath the bed sheets—but first I propped up an overturned picture frame on the nightstand. It was a photo of Victor and Carmen. I realized he hadn't mentioned her all evening.

"Hey, Victor? You think you'll get back together with Carmen?"

Victor cupped his hands behind his head, revealing two cottony tufts of hair beneath his arms—hair like I only wished I had.

"I don't know." He sighed. "I like her, but she's so jealous, you know? She's too clingy, too possessive. . . ." He turned to me. "Hey, what's up with you and Xio? She's pretty hot, if you don't mind my saying so."

"I don't mind," I told him, but it made me question: "Do you like her?"

"Not that way," Victor shook his head. "I thought you liked her."

"Well . . . as a friend I like her. But I can't decide if . . . you know . . ."

"Well, then," Victor said, "who *do* you like?"

The question caught me by surprise. What answer could I give him? I finally decided on: "I don't know."

We turned out the light after that, but I lay awake thinking about Victor's question—as I listened to his puffs of breath, so close beside me.

Saturday morning Mom picked me up and I said bye to Victor. I didn't really want to leave, but he was going to spend the day with his dad. On the drive home Mom told me, "Xio phoned again."

"Oh yeah." I realized I'd forgotten about her. "I'll call her soon as I get home."

But when we pulled into the driveway Dad was loading his car to go golfing and invited me to go with him. Then after he and I returned home Mom asked me to go with her to pick out some ceramic flowerpots for the patio. And while we were looking for those, with some Christmas money I bought a brass picture frame I really liked—perfect for the photo of Victor and me at Xio's party. After that Mom and Dad and I went out to dinner.

Sunday morning, when I came out of the shower, Mom said, "Honey, Xio called again. She said you still hadn't called her back. Is everything okay between you two?"

"Yeah," I said, but I was beginning to wonder: *Why didn't I feel like calling her?*

That afternoon I made ginger-mint iced tea from a magazine recipe and carried two glasses out to the patio where Mom was transplanting a pink hydrangea into one of the new, larger ceramic pots.

"Thanks, honey." She smiled as I placed a tea glass on the table beside her.

I sat down in one of the aluminum chairs, watching Mom carefully move the plant. "Mom? Um, remember when you said you thought Xio must like me a lot?"

Mom glanced up from the plant. "Yes?"

"Well . . ." I shifted in my seat. "What if I don't like her the same way?"

"Hmn." Mom pulled off her gloves and wiped the back of her hand across her forehead. "That's a toughie."

"Yeah." I nodded. "I mean, I like her, just not . . . you know . . ."

Mom climbed into the chair across from me and

sipped her tea. "Is there someone else you like?"

I thought about how Victor had asked me almost the exact same question. And I remembered waking that morning and watching him sleep, the fuzz above his lip shimmering golden in the sunlight. But how could I tell Mom about that?

Instead I said, "No. There isn't anyone else. But I don't want to—you know—hurt Xio's feelings."

"Well," Mom said, "she might feel hurt even more if you're not honest with her. Is that why you haven't called her?"

Just then the doorbell rang. That was weird. The doorbell hardly ever rang.

Mom's brow crinkled as if asking: *Who could that be?* Though I think we both suspected the answer.

"I'll get it," I said and hurried toward the door, trying to think fast. What explanation could I give Xio for not having called her?

# Chapter 19

## Xio

I'd spent all Friday evening wondering: *Why hadn't Frederick phoned me back?* What could he possibly be doing that was more important than *me*?

(Just kidding. Of course I didn't think that. Well, maybe for a minute I did.)

When I left another message Saturday and he still didn't phone me back, I really started worrying. Was he mad at me? Had I done something wrong or said something that hurt his feelings? I racked my brain trying to think.

That afternoon Carmen came over and we walked Stevie to the playground. (I'd forgiven him for intruding on Frederick and me, but only after I'd told him I'd wring his neck if he did it again.)

"Do you think Frederick's mad at me?" I asked Carmen.

"Why would he be angry with you?"

"I don't know. The only thing I can come up with

is: At school yesterday I told him his clothes made him look like he'd just stepped off a yacht. You know, that preppie-boy look?"

Carmen scrunched her forehead. "Why would that make him angry?"

"Who knows? I'm just trying to figure out why he hasn't called."

"Guys are jerks," Carmen said. "Victor hasn't called me for eleven days now. I don't care. He's crazy if he thinks I'm going to call him first."

At that point Stevie upchucked his cookies from swinging too hard—as always.

On the walk back home Carmen's conversation became all about Victor and how José had told him why Carmen was angry but he hadn't apologized, blah, blah, blah. . . . I wish she'd either get back together with him or just get over it.

Sunday morning Mami came to haul me out of bed. (I'd forgiven her too for treating me like some convent prisoner.) I rolled over, yawning. "Did Frederick call?"

"No, *mi amor.*" She opened the window shades, blinding me with sunshine. "Did you two have a fight?"

"If we have, it's news to me. Why hasn't he called me back?"

Mami gave a shrug. "Maybe he's busy with other things."

Oh, great. That made me feel special. I checked my computer to see if he was online. He wasn't, so I phoned and left a message with his mom *again*. Even though she was nice about it, I was starting to feel like a pest.

I went back to bed and lay on my side, staring at my Ariel lamp. I still hadn't called Papi back all these months. Maybe that had caused me bad karma and that's why Frederick hadn't phoned.

Should I call Papi? What would I say?

I brought out the note he'd sent with the Barbie. Slowly I dialed the number, rehearsing what I'd tell him. Would I have the nerve to say how hurt I was he hadn't phoned on my birthday?

"Hello?" A man answered, but it wasn't Papi. It was an Anglo voice. Had I dialed the wrong number?

"May I speak with Reynaldo Juárez, please?"

"Sorry, he's not home right now. Any message?"

Apparently I'd dialed the right number.

"Can you please tell him Xio called?"

"Oh, hi, Xio. Your dad's talked about you. He'll be happy you phoned. Is everything all right? Any message?"

"Can you just tell him I called, please?"

After I hung up I kept wondering, *Who was this man answering at Papi's home?*

As I helped Mami prepare Sunday lunch I told her about the call. "Some white guy answered. Does Papi have a roommate?"

Mami nodded. "He mentioned he'd moved in with a friend."

A *guy* friend? Why? If he wanted to live with someone, why didn't he move back in with us?

For lunch Mami had invited Rodolfo over. He brought dessert but wouldn't let us see it beforehand. "It's top secret," he told us in a hushed voice.

All during our meal Stevie and I kept trying to guess what it was, but Rodolfo wouldn't tell us. And when the time finally came, he made us stay at the table while he disappeared into the kitchen. Dishes rattled. Silverware clattered.

"What's he doing?" Stevie whispered.

The kitchen door swung open as Rodolfo's voice boomed, *"Damas y caballeros!"*

Like a fancy waiter, he'd draped a white cloth napkin over one forearm. Carefully balanced on fingertips was a tray of bowls—ice cream cake slathered with whipped cream, cherries, and sprinkles.

He served each of us, with Mami last. "And for the

lovely lady . . ." He lit a candle on top of her ice cream. ". . . Happy anniversary, Raquel."

As he sat beside her, Mami scrunched up her forehead. "What anniversary?"

"You forgot?" Rodolfo clutched at his heart as if devastated.

Stevie and I gazed at each other. Was Rodolfo joking or had Mami screwed up?

"I didn't forget anything." Mami giggled. "What are you talking about?"

Rodolfo's voice rang with indignation. "Exactly three months, eight days, fourteen hours, and . . ." He checked his watch. ". . . twenty-three minutes ago you finally agreed to go out with me."

*"Ay, que chistoso!"* Mami swatted him with her napkin, laughing along with Stevie and me.

Then Rodolfo reached across the tablecloth and rested his hand on Mami's. He wasn't just joking. It was obvious from the soft look in his eyes he really liked Mami.

She squeezed his hand in turn, the blush rising in her cheeks. Then her eyes darted at Stevie and me, and she pulled her hand away.

I sometimes wondered if that's why she hadn't become involved with another guy—because of us. Was she afraid we'd get hurt?

After helping clean up lunch I phoned the Sexies

to see what they were doing—and to ask, "What should I do about Frederick not calling?"

"Well," Carmen said, "maybe the time has come . . . to pounce! Make a move. Go over to his house. Get physical. That's what I'd do."

That might work for her, but I wasn't convinced that's what I should do.

Next I called María. In contrast to Carmen's confidence, her voice trembled with worry. "Do you think maybe Frederick likes someone else?"

Oh, great. I *so* did not want to hear that. María suggested every gloomy possibility I'd tried denying, and I began chewing the ends of my hair.

Next I phoned Nora, hoping she'd calm my rattled nerves. "What if María's right?" I wailed. "Maybe I should pounce, like Carmen says."

"Xio," Nora said matter-of-factly. "You can't make Frederick like you by pouncing. And stop listening to worrywart María. You just need to take your mind off him. You want to come over and work on our science projects?"

Do homework at a time like this? No way. Next I phoned José, moaning, "I'm so confused. I feel like my head's about to explode."

"Let's go for a bike ride," she suggested, "to clear your mind." That seemed like the most sensible idea yet.

We biked around the neighborhood while she patiently listened to me gripe.

"Am I obsessing?" I finally asked.

She gave a faint smile. "Maybe a little bit."

We both burst out laughing.

"How do you do it?" I asked her. "You're always so cool and sure of yourself—in school or sports. You're such a Capricorn. Nothing ever fazes you."

"Sure it does," she replied. "I just don't show it as much as you. I wish I could."

"Well," I said as we rode toward the mall. "I wish I was more like you."

After that I actually managed to stop thinking about you-know-who for five minutes. But at the sight of the movie theater, I started again.

"Why don't we bike by his house?" I suggested. "Just for a minute. We'll simply ride by. That's all."

José grinned like she saw right through me. "Okay. But then I've got to get home. Papá and I are watching a playoff game this afternoon."

As soon as she'd agreed, I took off faster than I'd biked all day, not slowing till we turned down Frederick's street.

As we approached his driveway I tried to detect some sign if he was home. Maybe he'd just happen to walk out the front door. But he didn't. At the end of the cul-de-sac I stopped and José pulled up beside me.

"Are you going to see if he's home?" she said in a low voice.

I kept my feet on the pavement. "I can't do that."

A moment later I was climbing off my bike in Frederick's driveway. "Aren't you coming with me?" I asked in a stage whisper.

"You go ahead." José pointed with her chin toward the door. "*Ándale!*"

I started slowly up the walkway. What if Frederick really was angry and didn't want to see me? I raised my hand to the doorbell. My legs wobbled beneath me. Maybe this was a dumb idea. Should I leave? I gazed over my shoulder at José.

"Just do it," she shooed me on.

My finger trembled as I pushed the button. Then I waited, sweating.

The door opened and there stood Frederick, wearing baggy shorts and a T-shirt, his face flushed pink. "Um, hi," he mumbled and offered a half-smile.

"Hi." I raised my hand in a wave.

"Hi, Frederick!" José shouted from the bikes. "Xio, I'm going!"

I turned, uncertain. Should I leave with her? Before I had a chance, she yelled, "Bye, Frederick!" And Frederick waved. "Bye!"

"Bye," I echoed as we watched José pedal away. Then Frederick and I turned to stare at each other.

"We were just biking by," I explained. "Since you hadn't called me back, I wanted to make sure—you know—are you okay?"

"Um, yeah." His face turned a shade pinker. "I, um, just got busy with stuff. I'm sorry."

It was then I noticed his neck was bare. He wasn't wearing the silver chain I'd given him.

"Um, you want to come in?" he asked.

After helping me park my bike in the garage, he led me inside the house.

It wasn't huge but it was definitely beautiful. All the furniture, plants, and stuff were arranged like in one of those design magazines. I remembered how during phone conversations Frederick had often explained to me about designs and colors and architecture.

"Your place looks great," I now told him.

"Thanks." Frederick started beaming. "I helped pick out most of the stuff from magazines."

He led me out onto the brightly flowered patio, where his mom was repotting a plant.

"Well, hi, Xio."

"Hi, Mrs. Jansen. You have a beautiful house and a beautiful garden. Everything is so beautiful. I mean it." Had I really just said *beautiful* three times? Fortunately she didn't seem to notice.

"Thanks." She smiled—kind of shyly, like Frederick.

"Have a seat." She gestured toward the aluminum table and chairs. "How were your holidays?"

I told her about my trip to Mexico, staying at my grandparents', and building the *Nacimiento*.

She smiled and said, "That was a very pretty necklace you brought back for Frederick."

The moment she said that Frederick's hand flew up to his throat. "Uh-oh!" He leaped from his seat. "I took it off at Victor's to shower. Don't worry! I'll call him. I know exactly where I left it."

As he darted into the house I brought a strand of hair to my mouth, chewing on the tips and thinking, *How could he have forgotten the chain* I'd *brought back for him?*

"You must like Frederick a lot," Mrs. Jansen said.

I quickly pulled the strand of hair away from my mouth. Had I actually chewed on it in front of Frederick's mom?

I nodded in response to her question, hoping she wasn't totally grossed out from discovering I was a hair chewer.

"Well," his mom said in a friendly voice, "we girls mature a lot faster than boys do. You know that, don't you?"

"Yeah." I squirmed in my chair. Why was she talking to me like some health teacher?

"And sometimes," his mom continued, "we can be

disappointed when boys aren't at the same point of development as we are."

Was she hinting something about Frederick and me?

He came back out just then. "Whew!" He plopped onto his chair. "Victor's mom found it. He's bringing it to school tomorrow."

"Well, I hope this teaches you a lesson." I wagged my finger at him. "To never take it off again."

His eyes darted between his mom and me, as if embarrassed. "Um, you want some iced tea?"

"Sure." I hopped off my chair. "I'll help you."

In the kitchen, Frederick poured me a glass. "It's homemade ginger-mint. I like experimenting with different kinds."

While we drank our tea, I told him about Rodolfo's dessert celebration for Mami. Then I said, "I really like your house. Where's your room?"

"Upstairs," he replied. "Um, want to see it?"

Of course, I'd hoped he'd ask me. I expected the room to be a mess like those of my friends' brothers—with clothes tossed and junk stacked all over the place. I figured I'd help clean it up. But his room was actually neater than mine. All his CDs, books, and DVDs were lined up. His desk and dresser were organized. His bed was made.

On the nightstand was a beautiful brass frame

with a party photo—but not one I expected by his bedside. It was of him and Victor.

"Where's the photo of you and me?"

"Um . . . over there." Frederick blushed, pointing toward the bulletin board. He darn well should've blushed. Why was Victor's photo in a beautiful brass frame by the bed and mine pinned into the corkboard with some cheap tack?

"I, um . . ." Frederick stammered. "I need to get a frame for yours too."

That didn't make me feel much better. *Why did he frame Victor's photo first?*

I tried to calm down, recalling what Nora had said about not being able to make him like me. I also thought about Carmen's advice. Maybe now was the time to pounce.

After all, we were alone, standing so close I could feel the heat from his body. The house was silent except for the hammering of my heart. I looked at the freckles on his nose, thinking I should've told him long ago how cute they were. I could almost feel the electricity between us. Could he feel it too?

"Frederick?" I whispered, leaning in closer. It felt as though a magnet was pulling me toward his rosebud lips.

"Um, Xio?" he replied in a quavering voice. "I, um—"

"Shh." I tilted my head to the right, closed my eyes, and brought my mouth onto his soft, warm lips. My heart turned cartwheels and back flips inside my chest. Emboldened, I slid my tongue between his teeth. He tasted sweet as mint, with a little spice of ginger. Was this a pounce?

If so, something wasn't quite right. Why wasn't he kissing me back? My tongue tapped his, but his just lay there. And even though I'd put my arms around him, he stood unmoving.

Didn't he want to kiss me? Was I doing something wrong? Why wasn't he responding? I let my arms slide from his shoulders and drew my lips away, opening my eyes.

Frederick stood rigid in front of me, his gaze focused on the carpet, his forehead damp with little beads of sweat.

I stepped back awkwardly, feeling I'd done something wrong. Had I been mistaken to kiss him like that? I knew you were supposed to let the boy make the moves. But what if he wasn't making them? Had that been what Frederick's mom had been trying to say on the patio? But what was I supposed to do, wait around my whole life for him to catch up?

"Um, you want some more tea?" Frederick asked and quickly grabbed my glass, stepping toward the door.

After getting tea we talked with his mom some more, though I can't remember about what.

As I biked home I tried to make sense of what had happened. Inside my mind I retraced our kiss (or *non*-kiss) . . . the framed photo of Victor . . . and a really weird thought crossed my mind.

Could Carmen have been right when she asked Frederick if he was gay?

*No way,* I told myself, pedaling faster and faster, the wind brushing past me as I tried to leave the thought behind.

# Chapter 20

## Frederick

I watched Xio pedal her bike away and tried to understand what had occurred. For the first time in my life I'd French-kissed someone—or at least, I'd *been* French kissed by someone. Any other boy would've been thrilled. So . . . why wasn't I?

I closed the front door and returned upstairs, where I threw myself onto the bed, thinking how I really, really did like Xio but . . . why didn't I feel more than that toward her? I wanted to be honest with her, like Mom had said, but how could I do that without hurting Xio?

I turned to face the night table. Victor smiled back at me from the brass-framed photo. I thought of him wrapping his arm around my shoulder. When he pulled me to him it felt so different from Xio—not only physically. It was something else inside me that I couldn't explain.

Was that crazy? Was it sick? I choked on the hard

knot in my throat, wishing . . . if only Victor were Xio and Xio were Victor.

Monday morning at school I was walking down the crowded hallway toward class when I heard a couple of boys shouting, *"Maricón!"*

I turned to see Iggy ignoring them . . . as he headed in my direction.

Since Thanksgiving, whenever I'd spotted him I'd managed to duck my head into my locker or disappear into a crowd before he could see me.

But this time I wasn't near my locker and the crowd was quickly thinning.

I wavered from side to side, trying to decide, *Should I ignore him?* He'd said I didn't have to say hi to him if I didn't want to. But hadn't I told him I *would* talk to him? Yeah, but what if those other boys down the hall saw me?

Just then Iggy caught my eye, breaking into a huge, dimpled smile.

And I turned my head away, pretending not to see him.

But as we passed each other, I sensed his gaze and my face burned with shame. How could I have turned away from him like that?

Disgusted with myself I shuffled on to class, remembering Iggy's parakeet and thinking about the

cage he lived in. It seemed as if I lived in one too—
except mine was invisible.

At lunch I wondered if Xio would act any different
because of our French kiss, but she didn't seem to.
Then I saw something I'd never noticed before: On
her notebook jacket was drawn a heart, inside of
which was written: FREDERICK + XIO.

The floor suddenly felt as if it was tilting beneath
me. When had she written that? I had to tell her
what was going on inside me. Except no way could I
tell her I might be gay. What if she told people? I
may as well lay outside the cafeteria doors and get
trampled to death when the bell rang.

Instead I'd simply tell her, "I don't feel the same
way toward you as you do toward me." Leave it at
that. She'd probably hate me forever after, but at
least I wouldn't be lying to her. And I wouldn't be
admitting I was a freak.

If Xio didn't want to sit together anymore after
that, I'd sit with Victor and the guys. I figured they'd
probably still be friends with me, since guys usually
stuck with a guy when it came to girls . . . unless the
guy was gay. All the more reason not to tell Xio that
part.

Now I just needed to figure out when to talk to
her. The bell rang. I pushed my chair away from the

table, and Xio turned to me. "Frederick, can I talk to you after school?"

"Huh?" I fumbled for my tray, a little rattled. Had she read my mind?

"I'll meet you at your locker," she said and headed toward the tray-return line.

During afternoon classes I kept wondering, *What did she want to talk about? Had she noticed I hadn't wanted to kiss her back? Or maybe . . . Did she want to do something even more serious than kissing?*

My breath started coming short. I dug into my backpack and grabbed my inhaler, drawing in a deep breath, trying to calm down.

After school I waited at my locker, watching students clear out of the hall and rehearsing what I'd say to Xio. My knees felt weak and my stomach woozy, but I was determined to tell her the truth—at least part of it.

"You don't look well," she said, walking up. "You feeling all right?" She pressed the back of her hand onto my forehead. Her skin felt cool against mine.

"I feel okay," I lied. "Really."

Xio gazed me up and down. "Let's walk outside."

In the fresh air I felt a little better. The sun was shining and a breeze blew down from the hills. The school buses had finished loading and were pulling away. Xio and I walked slowly toward the street as kids waved bye to us.

"Frederick, can I ask you something?"

My fingers tightened nervously around my backpack strap. "Um, sure."

She stopped walking and turned to face me. Her voice came out soft and unsure—barely sounding like Xio. "Do you like me?"

I hesitated. Wasn't this exactly what I wanted to talk about? Maybe that's why I hesitated.

"Um . . . of course I like you."

Her face relaxed a little. "Frederick, what I mean is . . ." She pushed her hair away from her eyes. ". . . Are you *attracted* to me?"

My gaze dropped to the sidewalk. How could I tell her no? Yet how could I tell her yes? My pulse throbbed in my temples as I glanced up again, mumbling, "I, um, ahem . . ." I cleared my throat as I struggled to force the words out. "I . . . don't think so."

Soon as I said it, I wanted to take it back. Her eyes turned moist and my breathing felt like drowning. What had I done?

"Is there . . ." Her voice caught. "Is there something wrong with me?"

"No!" I told her. How could she possibly think that? "There's nothing wrong with you."

She wiped her cheek, turning away like she didn't believe me.

"Xio, you're beautiful!" I insisted. "You're funny, you're smart."

"Then why don't you like me?" Her lip trembled and I could tell she was about to start *really* crying— all because of me.

"It's not you," I tried to reassure her, my own voice breaking. "There's nothing wrong with you. It's *me*, not you."

She sniffled, pressing her lips together, choking back her tears. "What do you mean?"

"I'm . . . um . . . I'm just not attracted to anyone, that's all." I averted my eyes and felt the sweat building on my forehead. "I guess I'm just weird." I glanced up to see her studying me.

"You mean you're not attracted to girls?"

I felt the resolve to keep my secret waning. Could I tell her the truth? I took a huge breath. "If I tell you something, you promise you won't tell anyone?"

She swallowed and nodded.

I wiped the sweat from my brow. "You *promise* we'll still be friends?"

"Frederick!" Her eyes grew wide. "You're scaring me. Yes, I promise. What is it?"

I closed my eyes for an instant. And upon opening

them, I put my entire future into her hands. "I think, um . . . I'm gay."

I'd actually said it. Exhaling a breath I hadn't noticed I was holding, I watched Xio's face slide from apprehension to confusion.

"But didn't you tell Carmen . . . that you weren't?"

"Well . . ." My throat choked up. "I think I am."

I watched a tiny stream roll down each of Xio's cheeks as my own tears started blurring my eyes.

"I wish you'd told me sooner," she said in a raspy voice.

I wanted to protest, "I didn't know!" But I didn't have the strength. Instead I stood silent, tears stinging my eyes, feeling like a creep.

"I'd better go now," Xio said, swabbing her cheeks, and turned away.

As she disappeared from view farther and farther down the sidewalk, I kept hoping she'd turn around. But she didn't. Could I blame her?

With the back of my hand I smeared my face. Then I headed toward home, wondering: *What on earth had I done?*

# Chapter 21

## Xio

As I walked home my mind churned through memories: how Frederick had tried to hide that he'd spent Thanksgiving with Iggy . . . how he'd become so hugely upset when Carmen asked if he was gay . . . how I'd always had to be the one to make the moves — either holding hands or kissing . . .

How could I have been so blind to seeing that (duh) of course Frederick was gay?

Arriving home, I slammed the door so hard the whole house shook. But I didn't care. Mami was at work and Stevie was at day care. I slid my backpack off and threw it onto the floor.

"You idiot!" I shouted, not certain who I meant — me for deluding myself or Frederick for misleading me.

Why hadn't he told me he wasn't attracted to me? Why had he let me make a fool of myself — especially in front of my friends? What would they say if they found out I'd been obsessing over a boy who was gay?

I marched to my room and hurled myself onto the bed. Now I understood why Mami hadn't become involved with any other man after Papi. Guys were dorks!

From my tear-damp pillow I gazed at the night-stand. The Ariel lamp's empty hollow gaped at me like a laughing mouth. Mami's words echoed in my mind: "You're the daughter he always wanted."

A surge of emotion welled up in me as my anger toward Frederick and Papi mixed together.

"The daughter you always wanted for what?" I cried at the lamp. "To hurt me by leaving us?" The anger rose in me as I sat upright, shaking. "I wish I could hurt you the same way. I wish . . ."

I yanked off the fish-printed lampshade, ripping the cardboard apart with my hands and scattering scraps across the floor. My whole body trembled.

"I hate you!" I jerked the cord from the wall socket and lifted the lamp base into the air. "I hate you Reynaldo Felipe Juárez!"

With one furious stroke I smashed the porcelain mermaid against the nightstand. Shards of broken china burst across the room, pelting my chest and legs.

I blinked my eyes shut and when I opened them

again my hands held only a bare pole and bulb
socket. I sent the metal skeleton bouncing across the
carpet, the cord snaking after it.

Then I flopped down on my bed and brought my
knees up, curling into a little ball of tears. Inside my
chest I felt my heart growing hard and cold and
closed. Never again would I allow myself to be hurt
by a guy. Never *ever* again.

Some time later I heard the front door, followed
by Mami and Stevie's voices, then footsteps in the
hall. A light tapping sounded on my door. "Xio?"

"Go away!" I shouted.

Of course, that made Mami open the door.

"Are you okay?" She peered in. Her eyes grew
wide as she scanned the scene. Scraps of lampshade
littered the carpet, along with porcelain sprinkled in
every direction, and my face dripped with tears.

*"Amor?"* Her voice rose with concern. *"Qué paso?"*

"Leave me alone," I sobbed, wiping my cheeks.

Mami stepped toward me, her shoes crunching on
the ceramic chips. "What's the matter, *cielito?*"

When she reached the bed, I flung my arms
around her waist, gripping her tight. "Nothing!" I
whimpered.

Her fingers brushed my face, pulling strands of
damp hair away from my eyes. "Well, something
must've upset you."

What could I say? Hadn't I promised Frederick to keep his secret? And for good reason. If people at school found out he was gay, he may as well be crucified.

Nevertheless I had to tell someone. The words bubbled up my throat and blurted out my mouth. "He's gay!"

Mami's forehead creased in confusion. "Who is?"

"Frederick!" I wailed, expecting her to react with shock, but she didn't.

"Did you know?" I sat up. "Did you? Why didn't you tell me?"

"*Cariño* . . ." She stroked my arm, trying to calm me down. "I didn't know. What makes you think he's gay?"

"Because he told me!" I heard my anger returning. "How do you *think* I know?"

Just then Stevie barged in the door, shouting, "Mami, I'm hungry!" But at the sight of the lamp debris he stopped short.

"Get out!" I yelled, turning my fury toward him.

"Xio!" Mami patted my arm and turned to Stevie. "*Papito*, eat a *pan dulce* from the pantry. I'll come start dinner soon."

But Stevie stood where he was, staring. "Why's Xio crying?"

"Are you deaf?" I shouted. "Leave us alone!"

"Xio, that's enough!" Mami shook my arm more sternly and told Stevie, "She's upset, *papito*. That's all. Now leave us alone. I'll be out in a minute."

Stevie backed out, wiping his nose like he was about to cry. Mami frowned at me. "There's no reason to treat your brother like that."

I crossed my arms, feeling more angry and mixed-up than ever. "I feel like such an idiot. Why didn't Frederick tell me in the first place?"

Mami got a faraway look, like she was thinking. "Maybe he was trying to figure things out."

I rolled my eyes. "I wish he'd figured it out beforehand!"

"Well," Mami said, "he probably had to work up a lot of courage to tell you."

I unfolded my arms, even angrier. "Why are you defending him?"

"*Cielito,* I'm not defending—"

"Yes you are. He's a dork! Guys are all dorks. Just look at what happened to you with Papi."

"What does Papi have to do with . . .?" Mami's gaze shifted to the shattered pieces of lamp littering the carpet. "Is that what this is about? Your father?"

"No! Yes. I don't know!" I was too shaken up inside to make sense. "I don't want to be the daughter he always wanted! I want to be cold and hard and strong like you."

Mami drew back a little and I quickly closed my mouth. Once again I'd hurt her. When would I ever learn? I lowered my gaze, waiting for her response. When she didn't say anything, I glanced up.

Her face had changed, filled with determination. "Xio, you're not me. And you're not cold and hard. You never will be. You've been hurt, that's all. And because of it, you'll probably grow to be stronger and wiser than I'll ever be. But part of being strong is learning to accept, forgive, and let go."

I folded my arms again, torn between wanting to believe Mami and being unwilling to let go of anything. Why should I forgive Frederick — or Papi?

"Mami!" Stevie had reappeared in the doorway. "When can we eat?"

"I'm coming, *papito,*" Mami answered and pressed her hand against my cheek. "Will you think about what I said? We can talk more later."

I breathed in her scent of hand cream and nail polish and watched her leave the room. I refused to think about what she'd said. I felt too . . . betrayed. I'd trusted Frederick and Papi and they'd betrayed me. Now I was supposed to forgive and forget? No way.

From the kitchen came the clang of pots and rattle of dishes, but I stayed in bed — till eventually Mami returned to my door. "*Cielito,* dinner's ready. I made chicken *mole.*"

"I don't want to eat," I grumbled.

Mami stared at me, her mouth turning in a frown. I stared back at her, unwilling to budge.

"Okay," she said. "Let me know if you change your mind."

I wasn't going to change my mind. I remained in my room all evening, ignoring phone calls from the Sexies, not wanting to talk to anyone. It would be impossible to hide how upset I was. And what could I tell them without snitching on Frederick? Instead I turned on my stereo and tried to drown the thoughts in my head.

It was after ten when Mami came in again, carrying a tray of piping-hot food. "I saved your plate."

"Mami, I told you I'm not hungry."

She ignored me, sliding the tray onto my desktop. "Well, maybe you'll want to eat later. Do you want to talk some more?"

"No!" I huffed. Even so, she walked over to me. "Then I'm going to bed now, *amor*. If you want to talk, you know I'm here." She leaned over to kiss me. *"Te quiero."*

I wanted to turn my head away, but I didn't. Her soft lips landed on my cheek and then she was gone.

The smell of chicken and chocolate sauce drifted

across the room. I fought to ignore it but my mouth watered so much my saliva glands ached.

Defeated, I shuffled over to my desk and ate every scrap of food. Then I returned to bed, exhausted.

# Chapter 22

## Frederick

The night after I told Xio about me I had really weird nightmares. In one I got to school and suddenly realized I'd forgotten to put clothes on. I stood buck naked in the middle of class, blushing from head to toe. Everybody laughed at me, so loud I wanted to cover my ears—except my hands were trying to cover my, um . . . something else.

As I bolted from class, my bare feet slapping against the hall tiles, I thought how stupid I'd been. How could I have forgotten to put clothes on?

I woke from the nightmare gasping and grabbed my inhaler. It took a while for my breathing to calm down. Then I went to the closet and pulled out what to wear for tomorrow, hanging it on my doorknob. There was no way I'd forget.

"Did you sleep all right, honey?" Mom asked next morning. "I thought I heard you in the middle of the night."

I wished I could tell her about everything going on. But how could I? What if she freaked out and . . . I don't know. I had no idea what she'd say.

And I didn't know what *I'd* say. It was all too much to deal with right now. Instead I just told her, "I'm okay," and drank my OJ, trying to act as if everything was normal.

During the walk to school, my mind verged on panic. What if Xio had told someone? Even though she'd promised not to, what if she had?

From outside Ms. Marciano's first-period class, I peered in the doorway. Xio's desk was empty. For a moment I sighed relief but then began new worries. Why wasn't she there? Had the shock of what I'd told her given her a heart attack? Had she felt so devastated she'd tried to commit suicide? I knew it was far-fetched, but it could happen.

All during morning classes I half expected the loudspeaker to crackle on. The principal would call me down to his office. Xio, her mom, and my own parents would be there waiting. Xio would repeat everything I'd told her about me. Everyone would shake their heads in dismay. The news would spread around school like wildfire and I'd be treated like a freak. As I walked down the hall kids would point and call me names, like they did to Iggy.

By lunchtime I was a nervous wreck. Slowly I

stepped toward my usual table. The girls were busily talking. *About me?* I wondered. Cautiously I pulled out my chair.

"Hi, Frederick," Nora piped up. "Where's Xio today?"

"Haven't seen her," I answered. "Have any of you?"

"I phoned her last night," María said. "But she never called back."

"Maybe she's got her *regla*," José suggested.

(*Regla* meant a girl's period, Xio had taught me.)

"She'd better not." Carmen laughed. "We're all supposed to be in sync. No breaking ranks!"

The other girls giggled with her. And I felt weirder than ever.

Somehow I made it through lunch. The rest of the day was like living in a movie—one where the guy murders his wife, dumps her body into a lake, and then acts as if nothing happened. . . . For a while he gets away with it. But later some unsuspecting fisherman starts to reel in his fishing line, and you know the murderer's about to get busted.

In class I sat on the edge of my seat, a total nerve case. I had to talk to someone. But who? I wasn't ready to face Xio again—and apparently she wasn't ready to face me.

What about one of the other girls? No . . . although I considered them friends, I couldn't tell them this. It had been hard enough to tell Xio.

What about Victor or one of the other soccer guys? Yeah, and why not also suggest they use my head as the soccer ball? I could never tell another guy I thought I was gay.

Except . . . maybe there was one boy I could tell. Would I dare to?

When the final bell rang, I headed in the direction of Iggy's house, sweating as I walked— either from the hot sun or nerves or both. Every few paces I gazed over my shoulder, paranoid someone would see me and figure out where I was going.

Meanwhile a million questions swirled in my head. What would I say to him? What if he wasn't home from school yet? Would he even speak to me after how I'd ignored him?

I almost chickened out and turned around about a dozen times before I finally got to his house. My breathing came hard as I banged the door knocker and waited, continuing to have second thoughts. Maybe if I just asked him how he knew he was gay, maybe I'd come to realize I wasn't.

The door swung open and Iggy's older brother stood hovering over me, mumbling into a cordless phone. His eyes narrowed at me before he shuffled back into the tile foyer, shouting, "Hey, faggot! It's for you."

From the stoop I stared into the house, newly

uncertain. Did I really have the nerve to go through with this?

A moment later Iggy raced from around the hall corner, slamming to a stop at the sight of me. Obviously I wasn't anyone he'd expected.

I forced my mouth into a smile. "Um, hi."

"Hi," he replied, squinting his eyes a little.

I shifted my feet, debating inside my head. *Okay, now what do I say?*

"Um, how's Pete?"

Iggy's gaze moved across my face, as if he was having his own inside debate. His mouth curved slowly into a half-smile, creasing a single dimple into his left cheek. "He asks about you once in a while."

"For real?" My breath popped out my mouth. "He does not."

"Yeah, he does." Iggy nodded earnestly, breaking into a full two-dimpled smile. "He says, 'Ruck-rick.' Want to see?"

The moment we stepped inside Iggy's room, Pete started chirping, twittering, and fluttering his wings. "Ruck-rick! Ruck-rick!"

"See?" Iggy grinned. "Told you." He opened the cage and Pete hopped onto Iggy's finger. Then he nuzzled Pete, puckering little kisses on the feathers. It reminded me of Thanksgiving, when I'd secretly watched his lips praying.

Just then the door burst open. "Hey, faggot!" Iggy's brother snarled. "I told you Mom said for you to take out the trash."

"Shut the door!" Iggy shouted. "Before Pete—"

Too late. The parakeet flapped its wings and took off, flying past Juan's head and out to the hall.

Iggy scowled at his brother. "You idiot!"

"He better not crap all over the house," Juan growled, heading out again.

"Come on!" Iggy yelled to me, bolting toward the door.

I tore after him, chasing Pete down the tiled hallway. In the dining room we circled the table, sliding, laughing, and trying to coax the bird from the unreachable chandelier. Ignoring us, Pete flapped toward the living room, zooming from lampshade to bookcase as we climbed over the couch, laughing even harder.

Then Pete launched toward Iggy's parents' bedroom, with us in lukewarm pursuit. Who cared about catching him? We were having too much fun. We bounced across the king-size bed, purposely bumping each other down and starting to lose our breath. It wasn't till the kitchen that Iggy finally enticed Pete with some cupcake and got a hold of him.

"Now you see what happens when he gets out,"

Iggy told me, gently stroking the bird's feathers. He carried Pete back to his cage. And I collapsed onto the carpet, still laughing, and drew a breath with my inhaler.

"You okay?" Iggy asked, sitting down beside me.

"Yeah." I nodded. His concern abruptly reminded me why I'd come to see him today. I stopped laughing and sat up, uncertain how I could go through with this.

"What's the matter?" Iggy said.

I darted a glance at him, trying to figure out where to start. "I'm sorry," I mumbled, "that I haven't said hi to you in school."

Iggy's jaw tightened. "That's okay. I'm used to it."

I sighed relief that at least he didn't resent me. I fidgeted with the carpet, tugging nervously at the weave. "Um, can I ask you something?"

"Yeah." Iggy straightened his back as if bracing himself. "What?"

"Um . . ." I swallowed the lump in my throat. "Is it true . . . what people say about you? I mean . . . are you really . . . you know . . . ?"

Much as I tried, I couldn't say the word out loud — not to another guy.

Instead I held my breath, waiting for his response. He stared silently back at me and I turned away, fearing he'd already figured out why I was asking.

"Are *you*?" he said.

That wasn't an answer! At least not one I'd anticipated. Why should I admit anything to him before he did? I considered the various alternatives for my own response before mumbling, "No."

Out of the corner of my eye I saw his steady gaze bearing down on me. "I'm not," I insisted. "I mean . . . I'm not sure." Slowly I glanced up at him. "I think I might be."

Iggy let out a huge sigh, his eyes softening. "Yeah," he finally responded to my question. "I'm pretty sure I am."

Suddenly I wanted to fly out of that room faster than Pete had. But I also wanted to stay and ask more, as a million questions swirled around my head, crashing into each other.

"How do you know you are?" I asked.

Iggy stared back at me like I'd just asked the dumbest question on earth. "The same way someone knows if they're straight."

I thought about how excited Victor and the guys became when talking about girls. Was that what Iggy meant?

"I think I've always known," Iggy continued. "People always treated me different—my brother, my dad and mom, kids at school."

"Have you told your parents?" I interrupted.

"No way!" Iggy shook his head. "They think being gay is a sin. At church our minister talks every Sunday about gay people burning in eternity. If my parents knew about me they'd probably send me for an exorcism."

Iggy crossed his eyes and made a goofy face, like in a scene from *The Exorcist*. I almost started laughing.

"But I know God loves me." Iggy tapped his chest, turning serious again. "I don't care what anyone says."

"So you don't think it's something bad?" I asked.

"Think about it," Iggy said firmly. "People have been picking on me ever since grade school—making fun of how I talk or walk—before I even knew what *gay* meant. I used to come home crying every day because of them. And they have the nerve to tell me *I'm* bad?"

His mention of crying made me once again notice the dark little freckle below his right eye, like a teardrop.

"It's who I am," Iggy said, his voice confident. "And it's my life, not theirs. The only reason other people stick their noses in it is so they can think they're better."

Hearing his anger was starting to make me think differently. *Why did people make such a fuss about it anyway?*

"Have you told anyone at school?" I asked.

"No, not yet." Iggy frowned, like he was disappointed with himself. "But there are some other kids I talk with online—a whole group of us in different places. There's even a girl in Alaska. Someday we're all going to get together and meet each other. And have a big gay party!"

He grinned and I laughed, leaning back.

"What about you?" Iggy asked. "Does anyone know about you?"

I told him the whole story about Xio, ending with how she'd been absent from school today. "What if she tells someone?" I sat up again. "What if everyone finds out?"

"Well . . ." Iggy nodded reassuringly. "I'll help you through it."

Our eyes met then, just like the first time I'd seen him. And as we looked at each other my skin started tingling and my stomach fluttering. Suddenly, uncontrollably, I was wondering, *What would it feel like to kiss him?* My face went hot, embarrassed by the thought.

As if reading my mind, a sly smile formed on Iggy's lips. And then somehow we were leaning toward each other, our mouths meeting. And in that kiss all my doubts and uncertainties seemed to vanish, replaced by a million possibilities.

It was a long kiss, and after a while Pete started chirping noisily.

Iggy pulled away from me, giggling. "I think he's jealous."

Before I left that afternoon Iggy and I exchanged phone numbers and screen names. His is **IggyBoyWonder**—like Batman's partner, Robin, the Boy Wonder. It must have stuck in my mind as I walked home, because every once in a while I stretched out my arms, as if flying. I knew Batman couldn't fly, but I felt like I was soaring. Except . . .

There was still someone I wanted to see—and make sure she was okay. I only hoped she didn't hate me.

# Chapter 23

## Xio

The morning after Frederick told me his big secret, I'd shut off the alarm and fallen back to sleep. Next thing I knew, Mami was nudging me awake. "Xio, you're going to be late for school."

"Can I stay home today?" I mumbled groggily. "Please? I don't feel good."

Although I wasn't really sick-sick, I couldn't bear facing Frederick and the Sexies. Not yet.

Mami felt my forehead. "You don't have a fever." She glanced over at the bare tray of chicken *mole* from the night before and laid her hand on my stomach. "Is your tummy upset?"

"A little," I lied.

Mami searched my face, gazed around the room at the lamp debris still scattered from yesterday, and gave a huge sigh. "Okay. But you need to clean up your room. Is that a deal?"

I nodded and quickly fell back to sleep, not

waking till nearly noon. Even then, for a long time I stayed in bed, watching the watery beams of sunlight stream through the window. I thought about what I'd done the previous day, trying to understand it all. Why had Frederick's news made me go so wacko?

As I lay in bed thinking, questions about Papi and Mami began crossing my mind—things I'd often wondered but Mami had never really explained. For example, why had Papi never remarried or even mentioned a girlfriend? My friends always complained about their dads' new wives or girlfriends. If Papi hadn't left Mami because of another woman, then why'd he leave? Was it because of something I'd done? Or . . .

A weird thought began forming in my head: Why had Papi moved to San Francisco? Why had he never let me come visit? Who was the man who'd answered Papi's phone? Could it be possible that Papi was . . . ?

A shiver ran up my spine. The thought was too crazy to even consider. I pushed it from my mind and climbed out of bed. Stumbling into the kitchen I found a note on the table.

*Buenos días, dormilona, ("Good morning sleepyhead.")*
*Hope you're feeling better. Call me when you get up.*
*Te quiero, Mami*

I picked up the wall phone and curled into a chair, drawing my knees up to my chest.

"How are you feeling?" Mami asked.

"Okay." I yawned. "Hungry."

"Have some fruit," Mami suggested. "Why don't you make a *licuado*?" Her other phone line rang and she told me, "Hold on."

While waiting for her to return I thought about the super-weird thought I'd had earlier. Should I ask her about it?

"Mami?" I said when she came back on the line. "Can I ask you some questions?"

But before I could get another word out, her other line rang again. Once more I got put on hold. This wasn't going to work.

When Mami came back on the line, I said, "Mami, when you get home can we talk about you and Papi? I mean *really* talk?"

"We can talk now," she said, but then her other line rang. "Okay, we'll talk when I get home. *Un beso.*"

After wishing her a kiss too, I took her suggestion and made a smoothie—slicing a banana and some strawberries, popping them in the blender with milk and a squirt of chocolate syrup—and carried the pitcher into the living room, where I spent the afternoon on the sofa, watching the dumb TV soaps and talk shows.

*Cristina* was all about celebrity break-ups, while on *Guiding Light,* Lucia confronted Alan about the truth about Gus. Oprah interviewed lovers who'd gotten caught cheating. And on *The Bold and the Beautiful,* Ridge told Massimo about Bridget's kiss.

Aside from the one phone call to Mami, I didn't talk to anyone else all day, not on the phone or online. Amazing, but true.

Around six, when Mami arrived home, I quickly started picking up my room while she changed into her after-work jeans and T-shirt. She prepared a snack for Stevie and told him, "Xio and I are going to talk for a little while, okay?" Then she came to my room, closed the door, and sat across from me in my desk chair. "So what's up?"

I edged onto the bed, facing her, and wedged my hands beneath my legs, steadying myself. "I want to talk about why Papi left. We've never really talked about it."

Mami shifted in her seat, crossing her legs at the knee. "Sure we have, *cielito.*"

"No, Mami," I said firmly. "We haven't."

She studied me, then ran her hands across her jeans. "Okay. What would you like to know?"

"Well . . ." I leaned back a little on the bed. "You've

always told me I'm the daughter Papi always wanted. So then why did he leave? Was it something I did? If it is, I want to know."

"Something *you* did?" Mami's brow furrowed. "How could you ever think that? No, *cariño*. He adored you. He still does."

"Yeah, right," I muttered. "Then why did he leave us?"

"Because . . ." Mami hesitated, as if searching for the right words. "I think your papá and I were never really meant for each other. It had nothing to do with you, *mi hija*. When you came into our lives it was some of the happiest time we ever had."

Mami's mouth turned up, smiling a little at the corners, but her eyes were sad. "Your papá and I were different, that's all. As the marriage continued, he began . . . slipping away . . . as if something was troubling him. I asked what was wrong, but he'd never tell me. His drinking became heavier. I suggested we go to counseling but he wouldn't. The more I pressed him the more he withdrew. I didn't know what else to do. I could tell I was losing him."

Mami took a breath, swallowed hard, and continued. "I hoped when Stevie was born things would get better, but they didn't. Your father said he needed time apart to figure out what he wanted.

What could I say? I agreed. And then came the divorce."

As Mami spoke her eyes had begun turning shiny and I felt like crying too. *Maybe I should drop all this.* But I couldn't. I still didn't understand why Papi had left. And my weird thought from the morning nagged at me even harder than before. But did I have the nerve to say it aloud?

"Mami?" I inhaled deep and braced myself. "You don't think Papi is gay, do you?"

In the silence that followed my heart thudded so loud I was sure Mami could hear it. Would she get angry at me for having suggested that about Papi? Or would she laugh at such a silly idea? I held my breath, waiting.

She stared at me with a curious look. "I asked him that once. He got furious!" The edges of Mami's mouth turned down. "Maybe he isn't. Or maybe he just couldn't accept it."

My jaw nearly dropped. Had Mami really said that about *my own dad*?

The room suddenly felt as if it was spinning. I gripped the edge of the bed to steady myself. "Mami, you're kidding, right? Papi couldn't be gay. Could he?"

Yet even as I denied the possibility, a part of me grasped at it. At least it was a way to make sense of why he'd left.

"If he was," I insisted, "why didn't he tell you?"

"Maybe he didn't have the nerve to face it." Mami sighed. "Or maybe he hadn't figured it out yet."

I felt an angry flush creeping up my cheeks. "Mami, I don't believe you. Papi is not gay! If he is, why didn't you ever tell me?"

"What could I have told you?" Mami's voice stayed calm. "I never knew for sure. Even now I can't say he definitely is."

"But you could've told me you suspected!"

"*Cielito,* you were a little girl. This is the first time I've ever mentioned it to *any*one."

I folded my arms. "I'm going to ask him. I'm going to call him again and find out."

I expected Mami to protest. But she stayed silent, making me wonder, *Would I really have the nerve to ask him? And what if he denied it?* At least Frederick had had the courage to be honest with me. But what if Papi never told me for certain? Or what if he *did* tell me?

My head began throbbing and I felt my throat choking up. Somehow Mami could tell. She walked over and wrapped her arm around my shoulder.

"Oh, Mami." I burst into sobs. "Why couldn't Papi have figured it out before he married you?"

Mami leaned her head close, whispering softly, "But then you wouldn't have been born, would you?"

"Yeah, but at least you wouldn't have—"

"Shh." Mami pressed her fingertips onto my lips. "I wouldn't trade you and Stevie for anything, *mi amor*."

I buried my head in her shoulder, sobbing. "Sometimes it feels like he took a part of me when he left—and no matter how hard I try I'll never get it back. Do you ever feel like that?"

"Sometimes," Mami said, her fingers gently brushing my cheek.

I swallowed my tears, wrapping my arms around her. "Do you think I'll ever get over wishing he never left?"

Mami gave me a long look. "Part of growing up means letting go of things we can't change. You think you can do that?"

I nodded though I felt uncertain. Maybe Mami realized that, because she smiled and said, "I think you can."

I nodded again, this time with more confidence, and squeezed her in my arms harder than ever.

After dinner that evening I was finally vacuuming the bits of lampshade and porcelain from the carpet, when over the machine's roar I heard Mami shout, "Xio? Someone to see you!"

I switched off the vacuum and turned, expecting to see one of the Sexies. Instead there stood Frederick, backpack slung over his shoulders, his head drooping guiltily.

*He should feel guilty,* I thought, glaring at him.

Mami's gaze moved between us. "I'll let you two talk," she said and left us alone, closing the door behind her.

"Um, hi." Frederick slowly raised his head to meet my gaze. "I missed you at school today. I came to make sure you were okay and . . ." He cleared his throat. "To say I'm sorry."

I leaned defiantly on the vacuum handle. Why should I forgive him that easily? "Sorry for what?" I demanded. "For leading me on? Why didn't you tell me you were gay to start with?"

He shrugged beneath his backpack. "I didn't know." He paused a moment as if choosing his words. "You helped me figure it out."

"Oh, great!" A new wave of anger rose inside my chest. "Thanks to me, you now hate girls." Annoyed, I flicked the vacuum on again and began shoving it back and forth across the carpet.

"I don't hate girls!" Frederick shouted over the motor's roar. He reached toward the vacuum handle, his hand landing on top of mine, and shut off the machine. "Xio . . ."

I narrowed my eyes at him and felt his hand tremble.

"Look," he continued. "I think if I did like a girl that way, it would be you, Xio."

I scowled at him, wanting to pull my hand away. "What do you mean?" I muttered.

"I mean . . ." His face had begun perspiring. "You're my best friend. You're fun and smart, you're funny, you're thoughtful and generous . . ."

"You make me sound like a Boy Scout." Even though I rolled my eyes I felt my heart softening.

"And you're hot!" He gave my hand a squeeze and gently let go. "I don't mean to me . . . but all the other guys think you're hot."

Now he was really overdoing it. "They do not."

"Yeah, they do."

"Like who?"

"Well, like my friend William in Wisconsin. I showed him your picture."

"Oh, great." I crossed my arms. "One guy two thousand miles away thinks I'm hot. I'm so excited I want to pee."

"Not just him," Frederick insisted. "At soccer the guys always kid me about you. I know they're jealous. They think you're hot too."

I hardened my gaze at him. "Really?" I asked.

Frederick nodded solemnly. "Xio, this isn't about you. There's nothing wrong with you. You're fine just as you are."

Maintaining my evil eye lock, I sat down on the bed and rested my chin on my hand, scrutinizing

him. Did I still want to be friends with him? *Could*
we be friends after all we'd been through?

I felt a little guilty for how I'd behaved with him. I
mean, I knew it must be hard being gay, just from
seeing how people treated Iggy.

"Well," I said, staring Frederick squarely in the
eye. "There's nothing wrong with you either. You
know that, don't you?"

Frederick gave a shrug that wasn't very con-
vincing. "I guess."

"Have you told anyone else?" I asked.

Without answering, Frederick glanced away.

That made me suspect he *had* told someone.
"Who else knows?" I whispered eagerly.

"Only, um, Iggy." Frederick blushed—as if embarrassed.

That struck me as odd. Why would telling me about
Iggy make Frederick embarrassed? Unless . . . uh-oh.
Another weird thought popped into my head.

"Is something going on between you two?" I
asked, my mind racing. "If there is, I'd rather find out
now instead of later."

Frederick turned even redder than before,
clutching his backpack and totally avoiding my
gaze. "I, um . . ." His voice quavered. "I went over to
Iggy's house today and told him . . . about me. And

then we . . ." Frederick cleared his throat and swallowed hard. "And then we, um, kissed?"

Oh. My. God. Would I ever learn to keep my big mouth shut? I sat in shock for a moment, then I leaped off the bed, slapping my hands over my ears.

"TMI, TMI, TMI!" I repeated, pacing the room till I was out of breath. Then I let my hands fall and glared at Frederick. "Did you have to tell me that?"

"Well . . ." He shrugged. "You asked."

I frowned, tapping my fingers on my chin, knowing I shouldn't ask anything else, but I was curious, too. "So are you and Iggy a couple now?"

"No." Frederick shook his head. "I mean, I don't know. It just sort of happened. Promise you won't tell anyone?"

His question made me recall the last promise I'd made to him—and broken.

"Well . . ." I sat down on the bed again. "I have something to confess . . ."

I admitted telling Mami about him and watched his face drain of color. "I'm sorry, Frederick, but I had to tell someone."

He stared at me, pale and wide-eyed. "Um . . . What did she say?"

I thought back over all the stuff Mami and I had

talked about. "She said it must have taken you a lot of courage to tell me."

"She said that?" The color bloomed back into Frederick's cheeks. "She doesn't mind?"

"I guess not. Did you notice she actually left us alone with the door closed? She probably figures you're now as safe as one of the Sexies."

I giggled but Frederick stayed serious. "You didn't tell them, did you?"

"No, but I can if you want me to."

Frederick's forehead knitted up, as if considering the possibility. "I don't think I'm ready for that yet."

Yeah, I could understand that, but it was going to be agony for me to keep it secret.

Frederick's gaze drifted past me to the nightstand. "Where's your lamp?"

"Smashed it," I admitted. "I got a little mad yesterday. But I'd outgrown it anyway."

"Oh," Frederick said, his brow furrowing again.

"What's the matter?" I asked.

"Well . . ." He began pulling off his backpack. "I'd finally figured out what to get you for a Christmas present?" He said it like a question as he zipped his backpack open. "I'd wanted to get you something really special but didn't know what . . . till that day I came over. Except . . . I don't think you'll have much use for it now." From inside the pack he pulled out a gift-wrapped box and sat beside me on the bed.

I tore away the wrapping, dying of curiosity, and pulled from the box a clock—just like the one I'd last seen six years ago, made to fit the Ariel lamp.

My throat tightened as I remembered spending countless hours staring at the clockless lamp, wishing for Papi's return.

"I didn't think they made them anymore," I whispered, my voice rasping.

"They don't," Frederick said proudly. "But I found it on the Web. It arrived this afternoon."

Two big teardrops rolled down my cheeks and splashed onto the clock's glass face, one after the other. And at the same time I wanted to laugh at the craziness of finally getting the darned clock a day after smashing the lamp.

"Um, are you all right?" Frederick asked. He raised his arm, hesitated, and then laid it across my shoulder.

"Yeah," I said and leaned into him.

# Chapter 24

## Frederick

Later that night Dad picked me up at Xio's to drive me home. I stared out the car window, thinking about all the stuff that had happened that day. Had I really told Xio about kissing Iggy? Had I actually *kissed* Iggy?

"You seem quiet." Dad reached across the seat and patted my shoulder. "Everything okay?"

I tried to decide what to tell him and finally said, "Just thinking."

What I didn't tell him was that kissing Iggy had opened up something inside me—feelings I'd never known before. Ever since, I'd been soaring in ecstasy, reliving every second I'd spent that afternoon with Iggy—chasing Pete over furniture, going back to Iggy's room, admitting to him about myself, and then my heart nearly bursting as we kissed . . .

For the first time I understood why other boys

acted so nutty around girls—their crazy excitement and goofy comments, their mixed-up expressions and kooky things they did.

It was a little bit like I'd felt with Victor—except with Victor I'd always known my feelings couldn't go anywhere. But with Iggy I stood a chance. And knowing that filled me with more hope and fear than ever before in my life. From out of nowhere, Iggy suddenly meant a lot to me. A whole lot.

"Did anyone phone?" I asked the instant I got home.

"No," Mom called from the kitchen. "But I made cookies." On the breakfast table was a trayful. "How's Xio? Did she like the clock?"

"Yeah," I said, taking a cookie. "Except . . ." I nearly began to explain about Xio smashing the lamp but stopped myself. Mom would probably ask, "Why did Xio smash the lamp?" Then I'd have to explain everything—or try to.

"Except what, honey?" Mom stared at me, waiting.

"Huh? Um, nothing. She liked it. I'm going upstairs now."

Mom gave Dad a curious look. "By the way," he asked me. "How's soccer going?"

"Um, okay. Victor said we're switching to softball tomorrow. Good night."

Once upstairs I quietly closed my room door,

dying to find out if Iggy was online. I hurried to my computer, then suddenly stopped.

As if a wave were crashing over me, Xio's question came back to me. Were Iggy and I now a couple?

I stared at the computer, asking myself, *What will school be like with him tomorrow—and after? Could I continue to ignore him now that we'd kissed? Shouldn't I at least say hi to him? But what if people began to suspect I was gay—and treated me like a freak?*

Did Iggy really mean so much to me that I was willing to risk that? Did I want to give up my reputation and my entire future in exchange for the daily jokes, name-calling, being made fun of, or even worse I'd surely get for the rest of my school years?

What could I do? Both choices sucked—either hurt Iggy by ignoring him or hurt myself by talking to him. And yet I knew that tomorrow or someday after, one way or another I'd have to make a choice.

Now I no longer wanted to check my computer. All I wanted to do was climb into bed and go to sleep.

I changed into my pajamas, turned off the light, and closed my eyes, but my mind kept racing. I tossed and turned the entire night, unable to sleep till the first dawn birds started chirping.

"Honey, wake up!" Mom shook my shoulder. "You'll be late."

I climbed from bed in a haze, the memory of the sucky decision I needed to make seeping back into my mind.

Downstairs Mom had set out my cereal bowl and milk, but I told her I wasn't hungry. In fact, I almost felt sick. Mom's brow scrunched with worry. "Honey, what's troubling you?"

I wished I could tell her, but it was all too much. Besides, what if she became overprotective, like with my asthma? What if she told me I couldn't spend time with Iggy?

"It's nothing," I said, trying to sound like I meant it. But my voice rang false even to me. "I have to decide something, that's all."

She gave me a long look. "Well, can you tell me what it's about?"

Nervously, I bit at the corner of my lip. "It's, um, kind of personal."

"Oh, I see." One of those annoying parent grins crept across her mouth. She probably figured my problem had to do with Xio. If only she knew.

"Well, I'm sure you'll do the right thing," Mom said, reaching over to fasten a shirt button I'd missed.

"But . . ." I let out a sigh. "How can I know what's the right thing?"

Mom gently cupped her palm against my cheek.

"If you're still for a moment, you'll know." She kept giving me that dopey parent smile. "Of course, it would help if you'd eat a good breakfast."

"Mom . . ." I drew away from her hand. "I've got to go."

All that morning my stomach rumbled. Mom had been right—I should've eaten something.

At lunch, all the Sexies asked Xio why she hadn't come to school the day before.

I waited anxiously to hear what she'd tell them, but she merely said she'd been sick and quickly changed the subject to the daytime soaps and TV shows she'd watched.

To my relief, the girls joked and gossiped as usual. Although I still felt like I was keeping a secret from them, the fact that at least Xio knew helped me relax—even laughing along a couple of times.

But after lunch I once again got nervous. I kept a lookout between classes, hoping to avoid Iggy so I wouldn't have to deal with my dreaded decision.

At the same time I hoped I would see him. Just thinking about a glimpse made my heart speed up and my forehead start sweating. But not till after last period did our paths finally meet.

I was walking down the hall with Victor and the guys heading out to the field. We turned the corner and there stood Iggy, chatting and laughing with a girl, just like the first time I'd seen him.

Wearing jeans and a white shirt that made his tan skin glow, he looked even cuter than in my memories. As our eyes met, his killer dimples crinkled in his smiley cheeks. And I was the happiest boy in school . . . but only for an instant.

Then Victor called to Iggy and his friend, *"Hola, chicas."* ("Hello, girls.")

The other boys burst into laughter at the dumb joke, flipping their wrists and prancing, imitating girls. Of course, they didn't seem anything like real girls.

Iggy's dimples faded and his gaze moved to me, his eyes angry but sad too, as if expecting me to do something.

I tried to be still, like Mom had said, while my heart sank. And in that moment I recalled all the times I'd walked past him, staring blankly in front of me, my heart aching.

Summoning every nerve in my body I now shouted to the guys, "Why don't you leave him alone?"

The words came out louder than I'd meant, echoing off the lockers. The boys abruptly became quiet and turned to stare at me. Even Iggy seemed startled.

"I don't think it's funny," I continued, my voice shaking. "He's a friend of mine."

Victor and the guys exchanged glances, as if unsure how to react. Then a sarcastic smile snaked onto smart-aleck Pepe's face.

"Ohh, they're *friends*!" He winked as if implying more than that.

Next Gordo asked, "You mean Iggy's your *girlfriend*?"

"Xio's going to be jealous!" Kiki chimed in.

The other boys started hooting and whistling, making me want to fold myself into a locker and disappear.

Except then I noticed Victor eyeing me—not laughing and cracking up with the others, but silent, as if studying me. Was he trying to figure out if my being friends with Iggy meant I was gay? Was he trying to decide if I was worth rescuing from the ridicule?

He rubbed a hand across his chin—like when I'd first told him about my asthma and he'd assigned me to play goalie. Would he now come up with some equally brilliant solution? Or would he decide I could no longer be friends with him and the team?

His eyes moved between me, the other guys, Iggy, and back to me. I waited, the sweat trickling down the back of my neck. Then Victor suddenly swung out his arm.

I blinked. Was he about to smack me?

Then I felt his arm swing onto my shoulder, like he'd always done, and he pushed me ahead of him toward the field.

"Come on," he told everyone. "Let's play ball."

I turned to see the other boys exchange confused glances. Why hadn't Victor made fun of me for being friends with Iggy? Did that mean it didn't matter to him? Was friendship more important to Victor than whether or not I was gay?

My mind was a jumble, not sure what to think. All I knew was the other boys were following Victor and me down the hallway. And that afternoon we started softball.

I wish I could say none of the guys made any more stupid jokes about Iggy or me after that day, but they did. In the hall, if Iggy and I were talking people would give us strange looks. On the softball field, if I struck out or missed catching a fly ball a guy would say something like "That was gay," and the other boys would laugh.

It took all my willpower to ignore it and not let them get to me — or to not say something mean back. Some days could be really hard. But I figured it like this: If it had taken me this long to accept myself, then I had to give my friends time too.

And I got strength from something: Victor hardly ever made jokes about Iggy or called things gay after that. Was it because he'd figured out I was gay? Or maybe he'd just realized how dumb teasing was. Maybe both.

Now on afternoons when there's no softball, I go over to Iggy's house or he comes to mine. We play with Pete, help each other with homework, do drawings together, or jump and sing to his karaoke machine.

I've wanted to kiss him again, but each time we've come close one of us has chickened out. I guess neither of us is quite ready yet to become a couple. But I think about it. A lot.

And I know one of these days we will kiss again— and just the thought of it makes my heart feel like a certain parakeet, free of its cage, soaring in flight.

# Chapter 25

## Xio

The evening Frederick phoned and told me how the boys had hassled him about Iggy I felt so mad I started pacing the floor. Then Carmen called.

"Did you hear about what happened with Frederick?"

"Yeah, I heard. I wish those boys would grow up."

"Well, is it true?" Carmen asked. "Are he and Iggy a couple?"

"Carmen, why are you asking me that?"

"Just to know," she said. "I figured he'd tell you."

"Well, it's none of your business," I snapped and hung up.

Why did people get in such a snit about the whole gay thing? I mean, what difference did it make if someone was gay?

My phone rang off the hook that evening. Nora, María, José, all wanted to know: "Is it true about Frederick and Iggy?"

And to each of them I replied, "Whether it's true or not, either way it's nobody's business. Now can we please talk about something else?"

Maybe part of why I didn't want to talk about it was also because I still felt sad things hadn't worked out with Frederick and me—as a couple, I mean.

When it came time for bed I threw myself onto my pillows and stared at the lampless clock Frederick had given me. And even without the lamp, I once again found myself thinking of Papi.

I hadn't called him yet and asked if he was gay, even though I'd said I would. The more I thought about it, the more I wondered, *What if that wasn't the reason he'd left? Or what if it was? Did I really want to know that? Would it make me stop wishing he'd come back?*

The fact was he'd left. Period. End of story. And nothing he could say or do would ever change it. Could I accept that?

I turned away from the nightstand, remembering Mami's words: "Growing up means letting go of things we can't change." And slowly I let out a deep breath.

In the weeks that followed my life returned to the dull, loveless routine as before the morning Frederick first arrived in Ms. Space Alien's class.

Until one morning a new boy named Adam showed up—with curly red hair and eyes even bluer than Frederick's, almost violet. He was gorgeous but . . . what if he also turned out to be gay?

Maybe I was being paranoid. But if he was gay, could he please figure it out before I got my hopes up?

A few minutes after sitting down he whispered something to Frederick, who shook his head and turned to me.

"Xio!" he whispered. "Do you have an extra pen Adam can borrow?"

With a weird feeling of déjà vu, I dug into my backpack and handed my extra ballpoint to Adam. Our fingers accidentally bumped and a little spark tingled up my arm.

Adam gave me a lopsided grin. "Thanks."

"You're welcome." I smiled back, trying to calm down and concentrate on class, but all I could think about was that lopsided grin.

After the bell he tried to return my pen. "You can keep it," I told him. "Don't you need it for your other classes?"

"I guess so. Thanks. Um . . ." He gave me that grin again. "You want my screen name?"

"Sure," I said, my face growing warm. I could barely keep still as he scribbled: RED-N-SWEET. I thought the name fit perfectly. I gave him mine too.

"See you," he said.

"See you," I replied.

"See you," echoed Frederick.

I suddenly realized he'd been standing beside us the entire time. "Frederick!" I said in a low voice as Adam walked away. "I *have* to know. Do you think he's gay?"

"No." Frederick gave a little laugh. "I don't think so."

"But how can you be sure?"

"From the way he looked at you. Xio, he was totally checking you out."

"No way! Are you making fun of me?" I leaned into him and could feel his ribs jiggling. "You'd better not be."

"I'm not making fun of you! I'm serious."

"Really?" We walked down the hall toward class. "Does that make you jealous? Be honest with me." I watched his expression to make sure he'd tell the truth.

"I'm not jealous," Frederick said without hesitating.

"You promise you'll tell me if you are?"

"Yeah." He smiled. "I promise."

That Saturday afternoon Frederick came over and

we took Stevie down the street to the playground. The two of them get along great.

While he pushed Stevie on the swings, I plunked down into a swing next to them and told Frederick how Adam had IM'd me and we'd chatted for more than an hour.

"He's a Sagittarius. That's a great Leo match, according to the love-signs book."

Frederick laughed. I knew he thought my astrology stuff was kooky.

"Higher!" Stevie shrieked, begging Frederick to push him harder.

"Don't push him too high," I warned, "or he'll get sick."

"No, I won't," Stevie argued.

I continued telling Frederick how Rodolfo had invited Mami and Stevie and me to go to Rosarito Beach with him this coming Easter weekend.

"It'll be the first time since Papi left we've ever gone away for the weekend with someone she's dating. I told her I think it's a good step."

"That's great," Frederick agreed.

And as he pushed Stevie I had this weird image pop into my mind: of one day being at the playground with my own little kids. I'm not sure where their father was—probably home watching football or something. But Frederick was there with me.

My heart jumped, the image seemed so real.

I wondered if it wasn't a . . . what's it called? A foretelling. Maybe it meant that no matter what, Frederick and I would always be friends. That we have something. That we understand each other. Or maybe it just meant I'm weird.

As I was thinking that, Stevie upchucked his cookies. I knew he would. He always does. "Time to go," I said.

Frederick grabbed one of Stevie's hands. I grabbed the other. And we headed home.

# A Glossary of Spanish Words Not Translated in the Text

*abuelitos*: grandparents

*amor*: love

*arroz-con-pollo*: rice with chicken, a Latin-American dish

*ay*: oh

*ay, Dios ayúdame*: oh God, help me

*ay, Dios mío*: oh my God

*ay, mi hija*: oh, my daughter (and *hijita* means "my little
         daughter")

*ay, mi pobrecito*: oh, poor guy

*ay, que chistoso*: oh, how funny

*un beso*: a kiss

*bolillos*: bread buns

*buenas noches*: good night

*buenas tardes, señora*: good afternoon, ma'am

*bueno*: good

*caca*: poop or doo-doo

*cariño*: literally, "caress," but used as a term of affection

*charro*: Mexican cowboy

*chulo/chula*: cute

*cielito*: literally, "little heaven" (a term of affection)

*curves*: curves

*damas y caballeros*: ladies and gentlemen

*este es mi amigo*: this is my friend

*feliz Navidad*: happy (or merry) Christmas

*fantástico*: fantastic

*frijoles*: beans

*furiosa*: furious

*glorioso*: glorious

*gracias*: thank you or thanks (and *muchas gracias* means
         "many thanks")

*gracias a Dios*: thank God

*guapo/guapa*: good-looking, attractive

*hola*: hello

*inocente*: innocent

*linda/lindo*: pretty or beautiful

*mami*: mom or mommy

*maravilloso*: marvelous

*maricón*: derogatory term for a gay person

*masa*: corn meal flour used to make tortillas

*mi amor*: my love

*mi casa es tu casa*: my house is your house

*Mole Poblano de Guajolote*: turkey with spicy chocolate sauce

*morena*: having darker-colored skin

*Nacimiento*: Nativity scene/creche

*niña/ niño*: girl/boy

*orale*: an exclamation meaning, "all right!"

*paciencia*: patience

*pan dulce*: pastry

*papi*: dad or daddy

*papito*: literally, "little father," but used affectionately to
mean "little guy"

*pico de gallo*: a type of spicy tomato sauce

*por qué no?*: why not?

*posadas*: Christmas caroling groups

*que chulo*: how cute

*que lastima*: what a shame

*qué paso?*: what happened?

*qué te pasa?*: what's the matter with you?

*señor*: mister or gentleman

*siesta*: afternoon nap

*te quiero*: I love you/I care about you

*tío/tía*: uncle/ aunt

*yo tampoco*: me neither